Henry Charles Banister

**Interludes**

Seven lectures delivered between the years 1891 and 1897. Collected and edited

by Stewart Macpherson

Henry Charles Banister

**Interludes**
*Seven lectures delivered between the years 1891 and 1897. Collected and edited by Stewart Macpherson*

ISBN/EAN: 9783337218614

Printed in Europe, USA, Canada, Australia, Japan

Cover: Foto ©Andreas Hilbeck / pixelio.de

More available books at **www.hansebooks.com**

# INTERLUDES

## SEVEN LECTURES DELIVERED
## BETWEEN THE YEARS
### 1891 AND 1897

BY THE LATE

## HENRY CHARLES BANISTER

PROFESSOR OF HARMONY AND COMPOSITION AT THE ROYAL ACADEMY OF
MUSIC, THE GUILDHALL SCHOOL OF MUSIC, AND THE ROYAL
NORMAL COLLEGE AND ACADEMY OF MUSIC
FOR THE BLIND, NORWOOD .

COLLECTED AND EDITED BY

## STEWART MACPHERSON

FELLOW AND PROFESSOR OF THE ROYAL ACADEMY OF MUSIC

*WITH A PORTRAIT*

## LONDON
### GEORGE BELL AND SONS
### 1898

# PREFACE

THE present volume consists of a collection of lectures by the late Mr. H. C. Banister, found among his papers after his lamented death in November of last year, and now printed for the first time. As these lectures were delivered on various occasions between the years 1891 and 1897, before audiences differing widely in their character and composition, it will be occasionally noticed that certain thoughts and pronouncements occur more than once in the collection in similar or, perhaps, almost identical language; but as there is, for the reason stated above, no intended *continuity* of idea between the various lectures, this seems to the Editor to be of small moment, especially as the excision of such passages would in most instances have completely marred the author's design. The Editor is responsible for a slight modification of the original text where the absence of the

musical illustrations, which Mr. Banister frequently introduced in explanation of his subject,
rendered this imperative.   Nowhere, however,
have these modifications been otherwise than
purely verbal; and, as a consequence, the
opinions and views expressed by Mr. Banister
—even where the Editor has not been able to
see "eye to eye" with him—remain exactly as
uttered by him when the lectures were delivered.

LONDON,
    *March*, 1898.

# CONTENTS

*The portrait is from a photograph by Mr. W. J. Wright of Upper
Norwood.*

CONTENTS

# INTERLUDES

## I.

## THE USES OF MUSICAL KNOWLEDGE

ONE of the most eminent authorities on education[1] has said to teachers : "First break down
the knowledge-idol; smash up the idolatry of
knowledge; frankly and fairly admit that the
majority of mankind cannot get much knowledge, and that any attempt to make them get
it is a manufacture of stupidity, a downward
education." And again : " Intellect-worship and
the banner of knowledge set up in a kingdom
mean death to true progress."

In harmony with this *dictum*, in spirit, is that
of another eminent writer and speaker :[2] " The
desire to know is an illusion. I do not say it is
a delusion, but an illusion. . . . We are never
more completely taken in than when in pursuit

[1] The late Rev. E. Thring.
[2] The late Professor H. Drummond.

of knowledge. Our idea is that we want the knowledge itself: in reality we wish no such thing. Men imagine when they go to classes, or join reading circles, that they wish to learn history and logic and mechanics and geology and chemistry. No such thing. That is the illusion of the spirit of learning, and it is a very beautiful and successful illusion. They are no more in pursuit of these things than the angler who spends a summer day by the river, and comes back with a basket full of trout, cares for the material product of his skill. It is not the trout he cares for, but the pursuit; and it is not the knowledge men care for, but the pursuit of it. The trout are edible and will count for something on the breakfast table; and knowledge is good, and its social and market values are not to be despised : and yet it is an illusion —a mere bait to make them do something else without their knowing it." And again, Ruskin says : " The real animating power of knowledge is only in the moment of its being first received, when it fills us with wonder and joy. Once thoroughly our own, the knowledge ceases to give us pleasure. It may be practically useful to us; it may be good for others; or good for usury to obtain more; but, in itself, once let it be thoroughly familiar, and it is dead. The wonder is gone from it, and all the fine colour which it had when first we drew it up out of the infinite sea."

Now, I can imagine that some of you may very well feel inclined to say, "If this be true, why call us together to hear a discourse on the *uses* of musical knowledge:" if, after all, it be the pursuit, the effort, which is the benefit, rather than the knowledge itself that is gained? And my reply may, at this preliminary stage, be that, while I wish to meet the inquiry so often put with regard to some branches of musical knowledge and study, "*Cui bono?* what is the good of it?" I wish first to assure you that there is a charm in the pursuit itself: I wish you to be enamoured of it, not merely for the sake of the ultimate benefit or utility of the knowledge attained; but, specially with regard to musical knowledge, with the methods of pursuit, over and above that which appertains to that process in other, or many other, departments of knowledge-seeking. I think it important that you be enamoured; and then the wooing will be to you like Jacob's seven years, "which seemed but a few days, for the love which he had for" his cousin Rachel.

For I confess that I have little care to speak to you in any mere utilitarian spirit. I speak to you as musical students, being myself a life-long musical student, and the first thing requisite to establish sympathy between us is that we be at one in this ; that we love music for its own sake, and therefore wish, at any cost, to know about her all that we can ; and then, I think, I may succeed in showing you a little about musical knowledge and its uses : its uses as matters of *interest*, not merely of gain, in any material sense. I assume this, then, as that on which we are all agreed.

Now, what do we mean by " musical know-ledge ? " knowledge which " is power ? " What is it that you are pursuing, and may intelligently pursue, as musical students ? What is the com-prehension of the term ? How much does it embrace ? I am not speaking of practice of an instrument, or of the voice, but of *knowledge*. I need not say anything about the use of technical knowledge of all that pertains to your instru-ment, be it what it may, in order that you may be thoroughly furnished with all that has to do, mechanically and technically, with performance thereon. No enlargement on so obvious a matter can be necessary, and all that is to be

said on the subject comes within the domain of
your respective professors. But there is a
somewhat prevalent notion among musical
aspirants—I do not apply the term "student"
to such as entertain this notion—that this special
departmental knowledge is all that is really
requisite for a performer ; or, at all events, that
other knowledge is so indirect in its bearings
on practical performance, as to be of but slight
advantage to those who only aspire to be in-
strumentalists or vocalists, that it may well be
dispensed with, especially as being as dry as it
is superfluous, and that the time and labour
requisite for its acquisition had far better be
devoted to additional practice of a technical
kind, vocal or instrumental. In other words,
that to be a pianist one need only practise the
pianoforte; to be a vocalist, only practise
singing, and so forth ; and the remonstrance to
the contrary would be met by the matter-of-fact
expostulatory question—shall I be any better a
player, or singer, as the result of any further
knowledge than that which appertains, immediately and directly, to my own department ?

I need hardly say, then, that the kind of
knowledge about which I am speaking, and
about which such sceptical and utilitarian in-

quiries would be made, is mainly that which comes under the broad and somewhat indefinitely comprehensive term of *theoretical* knowledge, with which, however, must be associated historical and some other collateral knowledge. But when I speak of theoretical knowledge I do not mean sets of rules. I remember a man, notorious rather than eminent, who made great pretensions to being above all things a contrapuntist. As a youth I heard the inquiry made concerning him whether these pretensions were sound and genuine. The reply was, "Well, he knows a great many *rules*." Now this is not what I understand musical knowledge to compass, useful as rules may be in some stages ; I mean knowledge of *music*, musical *principles*, *works*, and *structures*.

When Artemus Ward, at the conclusion of one of his lectures, pointing to a panoramic view of the Himalaya, said dryly : " If, as the result of all I have said, any one of you should be induced to attempt the ascent of one of the Himalayan range, I shall feel that I have not spoken in vain." I shall certainly not paraphrase his quaint irony. I do not desire that any of you, as the result of any remarks I may make, should become fugue-writers or composers at all. I should rather say with old John Cramer : " By all means let all musical students learn how to write fugues, all about the subject and the answer, tonal, real, authentic, plagal, the stretti, the episodes, inverse movement, augmentation, diminution, pedal-points — all about it; and then, when you have learnt how, don't write one!" I am not going to speak about the way to become composers, or the uses of theoretical knowledge to them ; that, I should think superfluous. But I address myself rather to the class whose questionings I have endeavoured to formulate, and, in addition, to those who, being earnest theoretical students, will welcome some suggestions as to the application of the knowledge which they are so sedulously acquiring.

I do not for a moment forget that the beautiful Art to which you are more or less devoted *is* an Art, rather than a science ; having to do less with facts to be known, than with emotion ; that it is a product of the imagination, nature's " highest gift," which " 'makes' a world that transcends nature, or 'sees' what in nature is hidden from the eyes of ordinary men." [1] But

[1] Principal T. C. Edwards.

one of my contentions, now, is that intelligence
and imagination should here go hand in hand;
and that understanding and emotion should be
linked, both in the interpretation and in the
enjoyment of our Art; I might add, in its
production, were I addressing an audience of
composers. A recent speaker, eminent, super-
eminent in his own profession,[1] that of surgery,
said concerning literature : " Intellectual knowledge or discernment was not necessary to a
comprehension of beauty. He doubted whether
any man admired the scenery of the cliffs and
mountains any the more because of his knowledge of their geology."

Now, I venture to think that there is some
confusion of thought here. To *some enjoyment*
of beauty, intellectual knowledge may not be
necessary; but to its *comprehension*—taking it in
—in any proper and full sense of the term, which
is one of fulness, surely " discernment," which
implies intellectual knowledge, is necessary, and,
where it exists, must conduce to enjoyment. A
geologist has all the same opportunity for ad-
miring the beauty of form, colour, and so forth,
of the mountain and cliff scenery, with the super-

[1] Sir James Paget.

added intellectual enjoyment of discerning the history of countless ages, which they reveal or indicate.

We are told on unquestionable authority that "knowledge *puffeth* up;" undoubtedly it does, unless there be moral qualities to balance it, which shall " *build* up." But while knowledge, especially "a little knowledge," "puffeth up," so does ignorance; a veritable wind-bag is the ignorance of a little knowledge. When Sir Sterndale Bennett was Principal of the Royal Academy of Music, some young men came to him as candidates for admission as students, and, with the swagger that comes from "advanced" thought-*lessness*, with the grandiose air of superior persons, said, " Ah, *we* go in for Wagner, and the modern school "—and so forth. Bennett quietly replied : " Far be it from me to hinder you from any explorations in any region of music; but let me ask you, do you know Mozart's Symphonies ? "

" Oh! ah! let's see, there's the 'Jupiter' that they sometimes do something from at the Promenade Concerts ; yes, we think we've heard that." " And you do not know how many he wrote. Do you know Clementi's Sonatas or Haydn's Quartets ? " and so on. " Oh, no! we

do not know anything about those." "Well, let
me advise you to make some acquaintance with
these, and similar acknowledged classics of the
musical art; and then come again to me and
talk about modern school, and advanced Art, and
all the rest of it." Of course I give not the
precise conversation, which I did not hear, but
the general purport, as told me by Bennett himself. It is this basis of musical knowledge, some
acquaintance with the classics, and with the progress of the art, proceeding therefrom, that I
would urge upon musical students. Think of
young people coming professedly to enter upon
a course of study, coming to learn, and pluming
themselves upon their advancement, and pre-
scribing to the Principal of their chosen school
what they shall learn, and where they shall
begin,—that beginning, moreover, to be a stage
of modern advancement. And people are considered to belong to the party of *progress*, who
think themselves in the van of advanced thought,
but who have made no *progress;* that which they
think they know being not their attainment,
but their beginning! Progress, forsooth! what
from ?

That which I wish to impress upon you, as
musical students, is, that there is a great deal

more to learn, a great deal more knowledge to acquire, than can be learnt or acquired by lesson-taking, however diligently you may apply yourselves to the deriving from the lessons that you receive all the benefit which they may impart. And you must take yourselves in hand; your professors cannot, in limited time, stock your minds with all needful musical knowledge ; you must try to compass so much about the progress and development of the Art as shall enable you to understand whereabouts you, and we all, now are in that evolution. You should, as pianists, for instance, understand so much about the successive stages in the development of your instrument and its precursors as to trace the expansion of the music written for such keyed instruments, from the older forms of *Partita* and *Suite* to the modern *Sonata;* and the reasons for certain forms of passage, and certain kinds of ornament or *agrémens.* This will have its influence, or should have, upon your performance, in showing you that any attempt to impart the largeness—mind, I do not speak of greatness, but largeness—of modern pianoforte music to the older music by adding octaves, filling up harmonies, and so forth, is an anachronism, an historical and artistic mistake, associated with the vulgar

·conception that a work cannot be great without being big; that much idea involves many notes, and the like.

Beware of thinking that, a century or two ago, the Art was in its infancy; or that those who then produced music were mere babes, or even—by a paradoxical perversity—estimating them as "old fogies." You see, or hear, or try to play, a modern piece of music, with many notes in a bar; perhaps very fine, but not because of its many notes. And then you turn to an old work with very few notes, and think it slender, and almost imagine that the composer did not put any more notes because he could not think of any. Rest assured that it is likely, rather, to have been because he did not need any; the few expressed his clearly-defined, strong ideas.

Did you ever observe, or think, how much there is, in small compass and with small show, in one of Bach's two-part Inventions, which you may have almost set aside as dry little exercises, and would have been ready to join with some one that I once heard say concerning the children who were *condemned*—mark you, not *privileged*—to play them, "Poor little things!"

But stay! I have to speak of knowledge.

Have you the knowledge requisite to discover the closely-packed thought that is in these? Will you understand the technical terms that I must use? A complete musical idea is termed a *Subject;* that you probably know. But when the initial idea of a composition hardly attains the completeness which is indicated by even a termination, or *Cadence,* or close, it is sometimes termed a *Motivo;* a germ idea, supplying the motive-power for thought, for working, for development. Now most of these *Inventions* by Bach start with just such a *motivo;* a little waif or stray, as it might seem to the superficial. But even as a waif in the street, passed carelessly by the unthinking, is a little jewel because of his soul, and will repay seizing and developing, so here.[1]    And, in this little phrase in two clauses—hardly that—is contained the whole movement,—as surely as the little egg not larger than a pin's-head contains all that is vital of, and is to issue in, the splendid butterfly which will delight the eyes, and which no art can imitate.    The whole movement is made of this *motivo;* only one half-bar, till the final chord, that has not this in it.    That which is

[1] Opening phrase of Bach's first two-part Invention.

true of the wonderful works in creation, that they "are great, sought out of all that have pleasure therein," is true, in lesser degree only, of works of human intellect, which are derived from the Infinite mind. But have you pleasure therein, so as to seek out that which is herein ? Now, of course, just as with any other waif, or any fragmentary thought, all depends upon what is made of it, done with it. How does it seem the other way, turned round ?

Now that turning it round, making an ascent for descent, and *vice versâ*, is termed *Inverse Movement ;* not to be confounded with *Inversion*, which is turning upside down ; though some musicians do confuse the two terms, using *inversion* to signify inverse movement. Now, this little *motivo* sounds well both ways, which is in its favour ; it is, so to speak, good on both sides.

Now, again, just as of a little waif, one may speculate, or even prophesy, as to what he may turn out when he grows ; so here, early in the career of the *motivo*, part—just the first four notes—are taken in notes of double the length ; which is termed *Augmentation*. You may say that to write quavers for semiquavers has nothing of special interest in it ; but then this is done in

combination with the original presentation, only
by inverse movement, like pointing to a little
waif, and while looking at him and recognizing
that he is a little boy, bringing in the imagination
of him as a man, in conjunction with, or contrast
with, his present size. And one gets accustomed,
as one goes on with the movement, to this
*augmentation;* and seems to make the comparison that one will some day about the grown-
up waif, and say, " Yes, I remember him as a
little waif, a little boy."

Now observe, further, that the second clause,
as I have called it, of this phrase, fits in with
the first clause, so that they can be sounded
together, the one being the accompaniment to
the other. And this fitting one part to another
—getting two phrases to combine—is just what
is meant by *Counterpoint ;* writing *part against
part,* or, as it is also described, " *the art of combining melodies.*" And you will also observe
that this second clause, *under* which the first
clause is placed, may also be taken, with equally
good effect, as the lower part, with the first
clause *over* it, and this is termed *Double Counterpoint,* which is simply an *invertible* counterpoint.

And then again, let me say, that this writing
one clause to fit in, sound well with, make a

good counterpoint to, the previous clause, is just what is requisite in the form of composition termed a *Canon;* the whole art of canonic writing consisting in writing that which, while it is a natural continuation of that which precedes, shall also be its natural accompaniment. Very simple this, as I try to put it lucidly, but not easy to do, I need hardly assure you.

So, thus far, we have had the *whole motivo* in combination with the augmentation of the first half of it, and then the second clause in combination with the first clause of it, by inverse movement. And then, as the movement progresses, that first clause is taken, in alternation, by the two parts, like a conversation, both by direct and by inverse movement, almost like *badinage*, upon one aspect of a proposition. And then the clause is reiterated,—taken by *prolongation,*—different from *augmentation*, and so, with modulations, changes of key, which are to the ear just what change of scene is to the eye and to the mind, the whole movement is carried on, with conciseness, cohesion, continuity, and completeness. Of this latter you can only judge by hearing it as a whole. And if any one urges the objection, which I have heard shallow people advance, that all this which I have been briefly explaining and illustrating makes no difference in the worth of the music as such, however ingenious and skilful it may be and is ; and is only interesting to those who know about it, my reply is two-fold. Firstly, that *knowing about it* is the very matter about which I am talking to you ; I desire to illustrate to you the interest of *knowing about it;* this is one of the " applications of musical knowledge." And, secondly, that the sense of completeness, fitness, finality, consistency, which, without your " knowing about it," may well impress you in listening to such a movement as a whole, results from the coherence, consistency, relevancy, unity of thought and purpose which characterize the music : it is intense thinking to a purpose ; condensed, compressed, strong thought. And my two-fold reply is like the subject of this invention, the two sections fit in with one another.

If you have had your interest awakened at all by even this slight sketch of *one* of these *inventions*, I can only say that there are fifteen of them in *two* parts, and the same number in *three* parts, and that there is no diminution in their interest.

C

I can understand, however, that some may, almost with a kind of revulsion, turn away from such an analysis, even in miniature, as this, and say : " Music is a matter of emotional enjoyment, not of logical study, like this ; and if musical knowledge means going into such *minutiæ*, and considering them like mathematical problems, I, for one, do not care about it." Well, it is of little use talking about knowledge to those who are not willing to think ; and that is why so many find theoretical studies difficult ; it is not because of the special difficulties of the study of *harmony*, or of *counterpoint*, but because they have not been trained to *think;* to think systematically, closely, and about that which is open to their observation. And one of the uses, to all of you, of trying to acquire musical knowledge, is that of mental training and discipline, in connection with a delightful pursuit and subject. Charles Kingsley somewhere says : " Study *something;* it does not much matter what ; " and surely it is most natural that you should make that your study which is to be your calling, when it is of so delightful and refining a character. And there is opportunity in musical study for acquiring the habit of accurate thinking, almost as though it were an exact science, in association with all the charm that pure imaginativeness will yield.

It is, moreover, with this, as with a country walk; with that it is a question of "eyes or no eyes"—that is, whether you have the *knowledge*, and the observant habit, which shall enable you to reap "the harvest of a quiet eye." With music it is not so much, or solely, "ears or no ears," but trained ears, together with a furnished mind. And however exuberantly imaginative any music may be, if it be worth anything at all it will yield reward for intelligent observation—that is, observation in conjunction with knowledge—such as shall place you in the attitude of mind which Faraday expressed when, anticipating a scientific experiment, he said, "Tell me what I am to look for." He knew, "prince of experimenters," as Tyndall has termed him, that without this previous instruction the very thing to be observed might escape him.

And there are a great many things "to look for" in music. One thing which may sound rather paradoxical to enunciate is "*the unexpected*," and one might almost unexceptionally apply to music the well-known assertion that "nothing is so certain as the unexpected" in

good music, with any pretensions to elaborate-
ness.    But this requires a little illustration and
elucidation.

Music is a language, and, like other languages,
has its punctuation, *i.e.*, its divisions into phrases,
sections, or paragraphs, and the like.    These
divisions are indicated, marked off, in music
by different sorts of close, or cadence.    Without
these divisions—points of repose, or, so to speak,
breath-taking for the attention—there would
ensue both strain and indefiniteness.    It would
be intolerable, moreover, were any considerable
portion of the music to go on without some such
terminal point as is analogous to a full-stop.
That we have in the *formula* termed the perfect cadence, or full close ; and that which is
termed the half close, or imperfect cadence,
corresponds to the semicolon, or colon.    In
one of Coleridge's essays, at the commencement of a sentence, there is a footnote to the
effect that the sentence does not terminate with
a full-stop till six pages later on, in order that
the reader's power of continuous attention may
be tested and exercised.    Now this would be a
great demand on the attention, were it at all
frequent, whether in literature or in music.    But,
on the other hand, it becomes fatiguing from

its monotony if that which is read be all broken
up into short sentences, even with semicolons
dividing them, antithetically. In this sense
how wearisome, tiresome to the ear—I say not
to the mind—is a whole chapter of the sen-
tentious wisdom contained in a series of laconic
axioms, such as the book of Proverbs. Now,
in music, one of the points of power and interest
is the sustaining power in conjunction with the
sufficiently frequent incidence of such less de-
cisive closes than the full close as shall give a
momentary fresh departure. To keep stopping
at the end of every four or eight bars, as in a
Psalm tune, or a ballad, becomes as irritating
as travelling by a train which calls at all
stations.

Now, among other devices for attaining this
continuity, and, at the same time, affording
agreeably disappointing surprise, is that of
averting a cadence or close, when it is expected,
a device known as an *interrupted cadence*. This
is neither more nor less than leading up to the
point when a final termination, a full close, is
expected, and then introducing some other chord
than that expected, the key-note common chord.
Examples of this device, the charming effect of
which is *felt*, where the process is not recognized

or understood, abound in the great composers'
works.   Apart from the surroundings, it is not
easy to feel the power of them ; and, therefore,
specimens are of little avail.   I may just cite
one or two instances, however.   In the Sonata
Op. 57, by Beethoven, generally known as the
" Appassionata," though *not* so termed by him,
the second subject commences in such a manner
as to give a full close, though in a modified
form, at the fourth bar.   When, however, that
same subject is introduced in the second part,
in another key, the cadence is averted,  three
times in succession, giving continuity in the
working.

Easier  to  understand  is  another  example
from  the  same  sonata, at  the  close  of  the  slow
movement, which, in fact, does *not* close, but,
the  cadence  being  interrupted,  leads  into  the
*finale.*

Another  example  occurs  in  the  last  movement, before the *coda.*

But these surprises, associated in such cases
with continuity, are not the only kind of unexpected progressions in music.   Unexpected
harmonies, in  place  of  the  more  usual, or  of
that which has previously appeared at the corresponding place, may be, and often are, intro-

duced at other prominent points.  Take, for
instance, the variations by Mozart on " Unser
dummer pöbel meint" (Gluck), in one of which,
at the resting note in each phrase, the phrase is
linked on to the next by the surprise passage
commencing on an unexpected harmony.

But now, speaking of these chords, I should
give them, successively and respectively, the
names of (*a*) dominant 7th ; (*b*) second inversion
of dominant 7th in the key of the sub-dominant ;
(*c*) first inversion of dominant triad in E minor;
(*d*) first inversion of dominant 7th in D.  And
while some might say, "Oh! I should never
remember all that, and those hard names," I
tell you that the knowing all these chords thus
is just the thing that enables me to remember
the passage.  This kind of knowledge is a
great help to memory.  Failures in memory
often result from its being mechanical rather
than intelligent.  A knowledge that a movement passes through certain keys, diverging
here by this chord, there by that, is like a chart,
assisting the mere memory of impressions.
And the same holds good of reading at sight.
A musician knows that such a chord is that
of, say, the German 6th resolving to the French
6th, and then to the dominant triad ; whereas

a non-musician has to try to remember that
the chord consists of D♮, B♯, F♯, A♮, and
so on. To the harmonist it is a word; by
the non-harmonist it must be re-spelt, or remembered in its spelling, not as a whole, for
each time.

And again, having been speaking of cadences,
I may here remark that the knowledge of how
to ornament with "cadenzi," cadence passages,
in vocal music—though I could well wish them
to be abolished, as they ought to be no more
requisite than in pianoforte sonatas—requires
acquaintance with the harmony on which the
ornamental flourish should be founded, and
how, therefore, it should be constructed. Forty
years ago, when I began teaching—nay thirty,
twenty—it was generally known among musicians that—I must almost bate breath in saying
it, true as it was—to be a vocalist was to be a
non-musician in the large majority of cases.
I think the reproach is not so universally applicable now; but I fear that it is by no means
obliterated, and it *ought* to be obliterated. For
anyone to have to say, I am a singer, but not a
musician, what a discredit it is! No branch of
musical practice should be carried on without
musicianship. To be a musician is to render

yourself independent of that worst of all kinds of so-called teaching which is called *coaching*.

I have, in years gone by, called on a Saturday to rehearse, as accompanist, with a professional vocalist, two or three songs for a Monday evening concert, and she has been obliged to say, " I cannot rehearse this one, for I have not yet sung it to Mr. So and So ! " Now this is a condition of things not to be tolerated, and, pianists and vocalists alike, the acquisition of real, sound, musical knowledge — theoretical, historical, and technical—will often now, and ultimately entirely, render you honourably, not disrespectfully or vauntingly, independent of your professors. You will, with such knowledge, not be constantly requiring your professor as a referee as to when to use the damper pedal, how to play certain grace notes or *agrémens*, ancient or modern, and whether such a note is a misprint, or whether it should have been marked sharp, and so on.

We in this school,[1] as in all such institutions worthy any notice, desire that you should be not pretenders, nor executants, vocal or instrumental merely, but musicians with competent

[1] The Guildhall School of Music.

knowledge for all that you undertake; and if you are to undertake tuition, rather than performance, however humble or elementary, how important that you should be thoroughly furnished with knowledge—broad, general, and accurate—to enable you to meet the score of educational *emergencies*, so to speak, which will surely arise.  I might tell you of all that has to be learnt about fugue devices, about sonata structure, about rhythm, phrasing and accent, about modulation and the importance in performance of due stress, prominence being given to modulating chords, and many, many other things.  I have sought more to stimulate your interest than to satisfy your inquiries, to suggest and to hint at lines of investigation and departments of knowledge.  Even as an eminent preacher discoursing on the text, " While I was musing the fire burned," divided his sermon by first speaking on the benefits of musing, and then trying to add fuel to the fire, so have I sought to show you some of the uses of knowledge, by briefly furnishing a very little, suggestively, rather than exhaustively, in the hope that you will go away, not so much saying, " Now I know exactly to what use to put each item of knowledge," as rather saying, with a pupil of mine, "What a deal there is to know!" There is, and it is worth knowing, and most interesting is the task of acquiring it. Do not be superficial, but determine, in the best sense, determine to be—knowing.

## II.

# THE APPRECIATION OF MUSIC[1]

As my subject is *appreciation*, I will begin by assuring you how highly I appreciate the fraternal feeling and artistic spirit in which you have honoured me by asking me to visit you, as a guild, and to address you on some aspects of musical thought in which we can all join, though you are following and representing a speciality in the diversified branches of our Art. Certain matters in the practice of our Art you know vastly more about than I. Other matters concerning the principles of our Art, it is possible that I have thought about more than you—some of you, at least—have had occasion to do. At all events, it is by each adding his quota to the common stock that we consolidate and weld the various items which go to make up the entirety—if that is ever to be made up—of musical knowledge and acquirement. I hope that your motto is : " Musicians first, organists after-

[1] Delivered before the " Guild of Organists," 1891.

wards." Because you count me as, to some extent, a musician, you ask me to come and contribute of my little store, and I gladly acknowledge the honour, appreciate the compliment.

Appreciation, be it borne in mind, is a much more comprehensive term than taste, susceptibility, impressionableness, or even admiration ; taking in all these, it implies also judgment founded on knowledge. It is defined, authoritatively, as "the action of estimating qualities or things, deliberate judgment ; . . . perception, recognition, intelligent notice, *especially* perception of delicate impressions or distinctions ; . . . adequate, or high estimation, sympathetic recognition of excellence." [1] Mr. Gladstone speaks of "the mental culture necessary to appreciate Homer." Hawthorne, speaking of another, says : " It requires a finer taste than mine to appreciate him." These two utterances indicating respectively the need both of natural and acquired appreciative power : the faculty and the cultivation.

And this may serve to suggest the reason of much non-appreciation, mis-appreciation, and shallow appreciation, if this be really apprecia-

---

[1] Murray, sub v.

tion, and, perhaps, of some of the over appreciation of music with which one meets.   That is
true in our relation to music which is expressed
with regard to the world around us in the
popular saying : " the world is to us very much
what we are to it ; " or that which is illustrated
in the story of " Eyes and No Eyes," and suggested by the very title of the book, " The
Harvest of a Quiet Eye."   Or again, since I
speak to a guild of church musicians, I may call
your attention to the general ethical principle
involved in words which you chant on the third
evening of the month: " With the holy thou
shalt be holy ; and with a perfect man thou
shalt be perfect.   With the clean thou shalt be
clean, and with the froward thou shalt learn
frowardness," [1] which expresses not only the
principle of the Divine dealing in the manifestation of His glory, but also the essentials, on our
part, to the right apprehension of all that is
pure, noble, refined, grand, in religion, in
character, in nature, or in art.

And, seeing that music is not a matter of im-
pressionism, merely, but also of Art in its " all-
roundest " presentation, not only of sensuous,

[1] Psalm xviii. 25, 26.

or rather sentient delight, but also of logical sequence, and of structural arrangement; and that it appeals to the diverse emotions of tenderness, passion, awe,—and likewise to the mental perceptions of symmetry, consecutiveness, coherence,—and so on : and then remembering how diverse are the emotional and the mental constitutions, whether natural or trained, among men, what wonder that there should be such diverse, almost contrary apprehensions or appreciations concerning the multiform varieties of musical composition. It is all very well to recognize, as Rossini did, only two styles of music, good and bad; that is a rough and ready distinction, hardly to be termed a classification, which may be made about a number of things, with very little discriminating aptitude. But even as in the pictorial art there is landscape, and historical, and *genre* painting—and, obviously, that is only one illustration among many that might be adduced—so with music. There is the contrapuntal and fugal style; there is the impassioned, declining all the restraints of that other style; there is the higher style, or combination of the two styles, which can express passion in conjunction with the restraint of structural law, more worthy of a rational as well as emotional being, of which, for instance, Mendelssohn's Fugue in E minor, Op. 33, furnishes an example; and I might go on subdividing. But it seems to be rare for the emotional and the intellectual to be so balanced in the same nature, and, moreover, for the same intellectual nature to be both *rangée* and *raisonnée;* and so we get one-sidedness, prejudice, and non-appreciation, in judging, or opining, or, in a way, appreciating music. It need be no discredit to any one that, with limited faculties, individual proclivities or habits of thought, he should fail to appreciate all kinds of excellence or beauty in musical composition, as in anything else. But it is a discredit that this non-appreciation of works and compositions which have won the admiration of the most competent judges at their own period should become positive depreciation with an accompanying tone of lofty superiority. It is this that would almost irritate those of more complete knowledge, of wider training, and fuller, broader sympathies, were it not that those who assume this lofty tone are known to be speaking of that which they so imperfectly understand. Moreover, there are certain fundamental principles of beauty and artistic structure which, if once understood, must silence the contemptuous banter of these self-sufficient critics ; and their scorn betrays their disqualification for the position that they take up.

In a notice of a literary work, recently, it was said of the author that, like another great writer, he " has his special circle of worshippers, who appear to adore his eccentricities as part of his genius." [1] And it was asked, " Is it too unkind to suggest that intellectual pride has something to do with this enthusiasm ? Delighted with themselves for being able to distinguish magnificent shapes in it, they are pleased to imagine their admiration of the intricate pattern is a mark of superior understanding."

Now we live in a period when, if it be not paradoxical to say it, eccentricity is a commonplace. I will not presume to assert this with regard to literature, to pictorial art, to various other matters : that is not my province. But do I err, or misrepresent the case, when I assert this with regard to music, whether in composition or in performance ? I am aware, of course, that the various manifestations of the tendency that I speak of are otherwise termed by admirers ; and that those who animadvert thereon are

[1] "The Times," -May 18th, 1891, p. 14, on George Meredith's "One of our Conquerors."

D

regarded as non-appreciative of that which is the very glory of these so-called artistic proclivities and productions. Unconventional, original, characteristic—perhaps daring, or weird—or sensuous, or fascinating, these, and many other such, are the terms used to designate, not to palliate, but to extol, not to disguise, but to distinguish, the kind or kinds of presentation which I have ventured to regard as eccentricities. In some other matters, such terms as sensational, or impressionist, or realistic, are used; and these terms are also applied to music.

Now, neither in music, nor in anything else, is it desired to move in a circle, always coming round to the same thing over again; turning musical history into a Rondo. But this avowal by no means disregards the necessity for certain central principles of truth, consistency, coherence, beauty, the which to defy indicates, too often, the lack of the training requisite to master them, if not of the basis of mental quality to perceive or recognize them.

But, dealing with the appreciation of music; is not the suggestion quoted just now applicable to many so-called critics of music, whether of that kind of great music requiring for its appreciation either special aptitudes, or qualities of intellect, or special training, or both, or of the modern eccentric, or, if you will, advanced, kind? With regard to great music, there is, on the one hand, the affectation of superiority exhibited in the *de*preciation of music whose pure beauty and real greatness its so-called critics are unable to *ap*preciate, from lack of native dignity of intellect or of knowledge, or of the discriminating faculty, trained by thoughtful experience ; and, on the other hand, the affectation of appreciation of that music which appeals not only to the nobility of intellect and emotion which characterizes the few rather than the many, but also to the culture which theoretical knowledge imparts. Of the first type of affected depreciators may be instanced those who declare—I will not say confess, because that would imply some consciousness of defect, some shame—but I say declare, without being ashamed, that they do not think much of Mozart. No, indeed, poor souls ! they do not think much of anything ; they are entirely unconscious of how supremely ridiculous they show themselves, and that they are too shallow to fathom the profundity, or too corrupted to relish the purity of one of the greatest of geniuses and of musical scholars; concerning whom, for example, one critic has recently said that "for all the subtleties of dramatic instrumentation, Mozart was the greatest master of them all."[1]

These are principally the younger generation of, I suppose I must say, in a qualified sense, musicians. It has been said to me by a lady— not professional—that at one time she did admire, or enjoy, Mozart; but that since the more recent developments of music, under, for instance, Brahms and others, she has felt the lack of satisfying power in the earlier master, though I am not under the impression that she styled Mozart a master at all; probably regarding him as one of the earlier students who might have done more or better had he lived nowadays. But still there was, I suppose, in her, and is, I also suppose, in many others, the idea, the assumption rather, that Mozart is obsolete; that we superior people have outlived all that. They think of that era of composers that they were, to quote Browning,[2] "stone-dead,"

"Because [they] lacked
Modern appliance, spread out phrase unracked
By modulations fit to make each hair
Stiffen upon his wig."

---

[1] "World," May 16th, 1891.
[2] "Parleyings," pp. 210, 211.

It is, perhaps, more fair than polite to complete the reference by adding that Browning terms those who talk thus "rash fools."

The other kind of affectation of appreciation is exemplified, for instance, nowadays, by the fashion that has set in of seeming to appreciate Bach.  I quite admit that, through the labours, before this fashion had set in, of Sterndale Bennett, and those who worked with him, the ice has been broken in this matter.  Some of you may not understand me in my reference to Bennett.  But some will remember that it was he, in establishing the Bach Society, now defunct, to bring forward, practise, and perform the music of the Leipsic Cantor, then unknown (with the exception of the 48 Preludes and Fugues, and some of the organ music), and in editing the six motets, with English words, and the St. Matthew Passion-Music, who really set in motion that tide of admiration which has gone on swelling ever since ; leading—long after the Bach Society, having done much initiating work, had been dissolved—to the establishment of the Bach Choir, and to the inclusion of excerpts from Bach's works in publishers' catalogues of popular works, as well as in programmes of popular concerts.  I was a member of that original Bach Society, which at least broke down the prejudice against the very name, as that of a dry maker of dry fugues; and people have become accustomed, reconciled to, even enamoured of, the very idiom which seemed so repelling, but was afterwards regarded as quaint. But let no one imagine that to be pleased with the delightful old-world rhythm of the gavottes and bourrées, or even to be almost oppressively overpowered by the Mass in B minor, or to be amazed at the performance by Joachim of the Chaconne in D minor, is necessarily to appreciate Bach. There is much in all this of mere dilettantism; and that will not do in the presence of Bach. Our coming back to any appreciation of his works does really seem as though, after all, music history was to be somewhat in Rondo form.

But I need not tell you that the intelligent, and the intellectual, more than—though not to the exclusion of—the emotional (as has been too commonly assumed), are the requisites for the appreciation of the marvellous productions of this master. It is absurd for those who know nothing of contrapuntal and fugal involvements to affect appreciation of, however sincere even their admiration for, such works. This qualification, however, does not stultify

natural enjoyment, which, indeed, there may be
without it.

But now, turning with relief from these petti-
nesses, let us think for a little of this very term
" the appreciation of music ! " What have we
here ? To appraise music sympathetically and
intelligently—appreciation, as has been said,
being " adequate, or high estimation," " sympathetic recognition of excellence," " perception of delicate impressions or distinctions," and
so on—what qualities of mind does this require,
seeing that the appeal of music is both to a
refined perception, a peculiar faculty, and to a
furnished mind, a trained judgment, a winnow-
ing power to separate chaff from wheat? For
there is the liability to be misled by mere-
triciousness and dazzled by glitter, which can
only be guarded against bv competent knowledge, theoretical judgment, analytical acumen.
And there is, likewise, the danger of coming
with theoretical bias, and of judging on purely
grammatical principles. For in musical composition of the highest order there is the two-
fold quality of genius and of workmanship. It
must surely have been with a very limited
intent of application, perhaps only to his own
art, that an eminent painter lately pronounced

that he did not believe in genius as commonly understood, only in special aptitude. Now special aptitude in handling a brush, or in mixing colours, or in the "composition" of a picture, undoubtedly there may be; whether there is genius in the conception of a picture, I will not, in antagonism to so eminent a judge, pronounce. But no "special aptitude" will account for one of Beethoven's Symphonies, for one of Handel's Oratorios, or for one of Mozart's melodies. There is the bringing into existence a creation that did not exist before; or, at least, a presentation of beauty, a revelation of it, from a perception which was more than an aptitude, a sensitiveness, conjoined with an interpreting faculty, along with, if you will, a special aptitude for workmanship, an infinite capacity for taking pains, which has been given as a definition of genius. But we do not speak of Beethoven, Handel, Mozart, as being better workmen in the symphonic, oratorio, or melodic craft, and by reason of their capacity for taking pains producing the "Eroica," the "Messiah," or "Non mi dir." Let the painter take this ground, if he will, and justify his contention with his brother artists as he can. But there is not a genuine musician here who will not ex-

perience a revulsion of feeling at the very
notion of thus characterizing the mighty master-
pieces of our beautiful art as results of special
aptitude, and products of boundless painstaking.
But, all the same, we withhold not any meed of
recognition due to that painstaking and apt
workmanship which manifest the artistic spirit
in the productions of creative genius. And
thus there are two subjects for appreciation,
which may or may not co-exist in varying pro-
portions, in music which presents itself for our
appreciation. I should prefer regarding it as a
twofold delight that is presented to us: the
appreciation of beautiful workmanship worthy
of a beautiful work.

It is by no means an infallible indication of
appreciation to have a certain liking for fine
music of a certain kind; while, on the other
hand, it may be a great mark of the power of
fine music that it can work its way through a
dense medium, and overpower even an unsen-
sitive and non-appreciative nature. With regard
to my first contention, it does not follow that
any one has appreciation of noble music because he is, in a measure, overpowered by
the grand sublimity of Handel's " Hallelujah
Chorus," or excited by the last movement of

Beethoven's C minor symphony, or by the peroration of Weber's " Euryanthe " overture ; or awed, or at least hushed, by the " Dead March" in Saul, especially when performed in the impressive circumstances which generally occasion its use ; or melted into some little tenderness of feeling by " I know that my Redeemer liveth," or by the first theme of Beethoven's Sonata, Op. 26, though it may illustrate the eloquence of music that can awaken sympathy in unrefined natures ; and it is an evidence of the inveterately hopeless flippancy and vulgarity which marks some natures that they can look round, and smile, and nod, and arrange for a meeting after the concert during the performance of the " Hallelujah."

But that which, in many cases such as I have alluded to, awakens some interest in ordinary minds is the rhythm, or the brass, or the " go " —for want of a better term—which appeal to some of the rougher, more commonplace susceptibilities of our nature. Appreciation, if it be, as has been said, *especially* " perception of delicate impressions or distinctions," is far more than this natural, uncultivated faculty, susceptibility, or whatever it be termed. And, to be not only this delicate perception, but also

" deliberate judgment, intelligent notice," it must be conjoined with, or the outcome of, the habit of observation which some training of a technical, structural, theoretical kind awakens; and this by no means implies that such appreciation is non-natural, artificial, pedantic, mere recognition of grammatical excellence : but such training cultivates the power of knowing what to look for, explains the reasons of certain emotional pleasures, surprises, and the like. Who that watches his own sensations, in other matters than music, does not know how much his pleasure is enhanced, or the reverse, according to the measure of intelligence that he possesses concerning the subject in hand? And this regulates and embodies his emotional pleasure; does not thwart, chill, suppress it, concerning any worthy matter. Is it not so, to give one example, to those who visit cathedrals, if they have some technical knowledge of architecture?

Is not this "appreciation" of music shown in the delicate perception of such flashes of genius as are exhibited by the simplest progressions, oft-times? Take, for example, so familiar an instance as that in the Introduction to Haydn's Symphony in D, where the first *motivo*—tonic and dominant only—on the return is given by inverse movement, tonic and sub-dominant. You and I could have done that ; it requires no skill, and nowadays it has become almost a commonplace, and we know what to expect— the chord of the sixth, Neapolitan or diatonic— leading, of course, to the $^6_4$ and cadence, perfect or imperfect.    But I shall never forget the first hearing of it when I was a lad, before the whole procedure had become familiar to me, how that low G seemed to take away my breath, and I looked round for sympathizers in my over-powered feeling and was glad to see the expression of delighted awe on the countenance of another susceptible listener—the late Robert Barnett.

Take another instance, Mendelssohn's Song without Words in F, No. IV. Book IV.    That diminished 7th on B♮, in the *codetta*, in that context and key, would, in the ordinary way, be resolved on tonic harmony, second inversion. What a surprise to treat it, as any tyro would treat it, in the first instance as a dominant to C, instead of as a super-tonic in F ! Cipriani Potter used to say, "Without being irreverent, I call that *a peep into Heaven !* "

Of course, I am not insinuating that the

members of this guild are not quite as capable as I of thus analyzing progressions of this kind; but I take the opportunity of calling your attention to them as germane to my subject. They indicate that delicate appreciation of the most exquisite affinities in music: a most precious form of appreciation; and it is just because of the rare delicacy of such passages as these that they are not appreciated unless there be the theoretical training which enables one to analyze and understand. I repeat, emphatically, that their charm to us as theoretical musicians, does not lie in their being theoretical nuts, cracked or to crack, but in the delicious kernels, which we could only hear shaking about till we cracked the nuts. We do not gloat over the shells, but are glad to know how to crack them. We do not cite such extracts as these and appreciate them because they are clever; it is not a matter of cleverness at all, but it is the exquisite instinct which our theoretical knowledge enables us to detect that we, I trust, appreciate. For my own part I confess that I am out of heart with "clever" music, and am half inclined to mis-apply, that is, to apply in a different sense from that which was in Kingsley's mind, his injunction to the little girl: "Be good, sweet

maid, and let who will be clever." Lord Bacon
says : " I think a Painter may make a better
Face than ever was ; but he must do it by a
kind of Felicity (as a Musician that maketh an
excellent Air in Musick), and not by Rule." [1]
Yes, rules are good for students, but we do not
appreciate music for its observance of or subservience to rule ; we appreciate the "kind of
felicity " such as these beautiful quotations exemplify.

If it be true, however, that under the influence
of music the soul of a genius "looks out through
renovated eyes ;" that in certain of its moods
its power is such that,

> "The soul delighted on each accent dwells,—
> Enraptured dwells,—not daring to respire ;"

that,

> "Wild warblings from the Æolian lyre,
> Enchantments softly breathe, and tremblingly expire ;"

that it has power to " melt the soul to pity and
to love," and yet that there is a method in all
this delightful emotional power ; that music calls
forth such logical and structural acumen as the
great contrapuntal works exemplify ; that it
allies itself at once with each and all our varied

[1] Essay on Beauty.

emotions and with all our intellectual strength, lending itself, sympathetically, to the playfulness of the child, the tenderness of the lover, to martial fire, to religious fervour, to ratiocinative elaboration, and need suffer no corruption in any of these and other alliances ; how shall I go on to speak of appreciating it ? It is even one form, one may say, of the wisdom whose " price is above rubies." At least to me it is so, as my solace and sunshine. May it ever be with me that the love of God comes first; then human love sanctified by that; and the love of music, not third, but as the refining influence pervading, and in conjunction with, both; all three may I ever retain. This fervent desire sufficiently indicates my personal " appreciation of music."

# III
## MUSIC AND PREACHING[1]

I AM asked to address you on some matters concerning the art of music, which I follow as my profession, and for the time being represent, and the theological studies which you religiously pursue, or, at least, on some points of contact and of sympathy which may be supposed to be discoverable between us in our seemingly very dissimilar callings. The term " border-line " was used by your Principal when he broached the subject to me, implying that in some sense, mental or moral, intellectual or spiritual, or both, we are very near neighbours; so near as to be able to look one another in the face, exchange thoughts in perhaps somewhat of a mixed dialect, our atmosphere being, in the border region, one; it is not a gulf, hardly a stream, that divides us, only an imaginary line, a sort of geographical expression.   Is there really this

[1] Delivered before the students of Hackney Theological College, 1891.

affinity between us ? To what extent you are in sympathy with me in my art, or find any affinity between our pursuits, between that which is termed "the Queen of Sciences," theology, and "Music, heavenly maid," I am unable to judge just now. It will be in vain, however, for me to speak to you this evening, unless I succeed in enlisting your sympathy and in kindling your interest, and even in awakening some new thoughts and impressions concerning music which shall exercise a refining reflex influence upon you, and so tell somewhat upon your studies and future work. And I say all this, not, as you might suppose, because of a lack of apprehension concerning your pursuits, with which, on the contrary, I trust that I may, without presumption, venture to say that I am in full and not unintelligent sympathy. For, to make at once the only personal reference which I obtrude upon you, I may tell you that for not far short of forty years I have been more or less intensely interested and occupied in theological study and in preaching work. The two lines of thought and occupation have run parallel in my mind and life during that period ; so that I am not ignorant as to your work, present and future, and I have found much sweetness and

E

strength, personally, from the twofold course of
work and thought in my own case.   As Bishop
Beveridge said :  " When  music  sounds  the
sweetest in  my ears, truth commonly flows the
clearest into my mind ; and hence it is that I
find my soul is becoming more harmonious by
being accustomed so much to harmony."

I do not think that there is any irreverence
in extending the range of application of that
Apostolic pronouncement concerning the precious stewardship in charge of those who are
" put in trust with the gospel ; " " we have this
treasure in earthen vessels, that the excellency
of the power may be of God."   Every perception of, or intuition for the beautiful and refined
is, even if in an infinitely less degree, as well as
of different kind, a treasure from the Divine
treasury, deposited in an earthen vessel, for the
awakening from grossness, the refinement of
one's fellow men, and is, truly, a spark from the
Divine fire, a revelation by that same Spirit Who
" distributeth to every man severally as He
will ; " " it cometh from the Lord of hosts, which
is wonderful in counsel and excellent in wisdom ;"[1]
the same God who " doth instruct aright and
teach" the ploughman, the agriculturist, con-

[1] Isa. xxviii. 23-29 (R.V.).

cerning "sowing" and "breaking the clods,
casting abroad the fitches, scattering the cum-
min," and so on, and who "put wisdom and
understanding to know how to work,"[1] cunningly
to "devise," into the hearts of Bezaleel and
Oholiab, who still gives these several faculties,
and, further and specially, over and beyond the
general mental faculty, cunning, wisdom, understanding, with or without a particular bent for
its application. When that unique artistic
faculty, the power to, as we say, originate and
express in artistic fashion, as in music, a
beautiful idea, is given, that is a revelation of
beauty, not merely a use to which the mental
faculties generally are put—the devising and
making, producing, that which did not exist
before—but the receiving and being the channel
of communication from the Divine mind of a
little of the beauty therein dwelling; an emanation from the mind in which all purity and
grace and beauty are immanent; it is not a
human device but a Divine "treasure in an
earthen vessel." "Doubtless all the creatures,
in their several ranks, have some . . . impresses
from the Creator, by which His transcendent
perfections may be somewhat observed. That

[1] Exod. xxxvi. 1, 2 (R.V.).

God is now so communicative as to give to all
creatures in the world whatever Being, Motion,
Life, Order, Beauty, Harmony, Reason, Grace,
Glory, any of them possess, is past all question to considering, sober reason." [1]   Of such
a beautiful idea, more or less fitly expressed
artistically, which is commonly called a product
of genius, the language might be used by the
human interpreter with the substitution of the
term "beauty" for "love" :

> "The love within my heart for thee
>   Before the world was had its birth,
> It is the part God gives to me
>   Of the great wisdom of the earth." [2]

So that the denial of genius is of the nature of
atheism : a denial that beauty is a revelation
from the Divine originator, regarding it as a
discovery or invention, or manufacture by
human intellect.

Pray do not credit me, however, with the
shallow confusion of thought which eviscerates
the authority of Holy Scripture by reducing its
inspiration to a level with that of wor ks of

[1] R. Baxter, "Knowledge and Love compared," 1689,
296-297.
[2] "A Light Load," by Dollie Radford. "Academy,"
June 13th, 1891.

human genius. These, in literature, profess not to reveal new truths; but either exercise intellect on accepted truths or visible things, at best discovering neglected or overlooked truths; or, by the exercise of imagination, suggest new subjects of thought, and soar above the gross and the material. But it will ever remain that " Eye hath not seen, nor ear heard, nor heart of man conceived, the things that God hath prepared for them that love Him;" but God hath revealed them to men by His Spirit (holy men of old spake of these, as they were moved by that Holy Spirit). All I contend for is that a beautiful musical thought, especially, is not, in its germ, an evolvement, but a reception, the prize of a specially receptive faculty, that listens, as it were, for the music, not of the spheres indeed, but of the hidden world of beauty, in which the beauty of the Lord is manifest. I cannot put it more plainly. Genius has indeed been called the "infinite capacity for taking pains," but all the painstaking in the world will never produce an oratorio like the " Messiah " or " Elijah." The painstaking comes afterwards in working out the germ idea. As a matter of fact, indeed, the " Messiah," like some others of Handel's

works, being written in about a month, could
not have been the result of much painstaking.
But there needs, as a rule, prior and subsequent
painstaking to prepare the earthen vessel to
receive the treasure, and then to develop and
express it in fitting manner.   So that it was not
far from the truth when my old master, Cipriani
Potter, said, concerning a particular chord in
one of Mendelssohn's " Lieder," " that is a peep
into Heaven !" a remark that he made also, if I
remember rightly, about the theme of the slow
movement of Beethoven's "Kreutzer" sonata.

A preacher and writer[1]—one of your own
order—has averred that " men are wont to
regard a skilful musician with a sentiment akin
to worship.   That any person should be able
to play several parts on a pipe organ with hands
and feet, and at the same time read the notes
and the words and sing, is truly astonishing,
and comes, perhaps, as near Divine action as
any mere man is capable of doing."

I may remark, in passing, that the experience
of organists by no means tallies with this aver-
ment.  Especially would they say that ministers,
clergymen, are not at all in the habit of regard-

---

[1] Rev. E. C. Lawrence, Ph.D.  "Freeman," Sept. 18th,
1891.

ing them as such very superior, almost super-
natural persons; they are often treated rather
as very subordinate persons indeed to the
parsons themselves : but let that pass.   I make
the quotation because it illustrates a vulgar
apprehension as to what constitutes a superior
musician, as to wherein and wherefore musicianship is worthy of special honour, in mechanical
dexterity, forsooth, in being able to play so
many notes at a time, and with hands and feet
simultaneously, possibly with the voice in use at
the same time ! Whereas this part of a musician's
work, though important, is really largely a matter
of training, to such an extent as that the mechanical action becomes almost automatic ; the
eye sees, sends word to the brain, the brain
sends word to the fingers and the feet, the
voluntary muscles being set to work.   Wonderful, truly ! as all that is connected with our
nervous and muscular system.   But all that is
not necessarily *musical* faculty at all; though
the true musical perception, intuition, knowledge, brought into co-operative play, make all
the difference, even with respect to the complex
mechanical procedure.   The same writer goes
on to say : "Some scholars believe that the
planets are set at intervals corresponding to the

scale in music, and that in their movements
they are so attuned as to produce 'the music of
the spheres,' but that the celestial concert is
only enjoyed by angels and other superior
beings, the ears of man being too gross for such
Divine melody." I make this additional quotation as a warning to preachers, and any others
whom it may concern, against talking nonsense
through venturing to talk about that which they
do not understand, a warning specially needful
to preachers when they talk about music.

How common, for instance, for preachers to
talk about the minor key or mode as though it
necessarily implied, was almost a synonym for,
that which is sad or melancholy, whereas the
well-known song of Handel's, " O ruddier than
the cherry," not at all sad, is in the minor
mode ; while one of the most solemn of threno-
dies, the "Dead March" in "Saul," is in the
major mode. And so they talk, sometimes as
though *discord* necessarily implied disagree-
ableness; whereas it merely means a combination which is non-reposeful, but requires and
suggests another combination to follow it, which
is technically termed *Resolution.*

One who would not, perhaps, be credited
with the softer and more refined emotions—

rather with the sterner views of life and doctrine
—has said : " Amongst other things which are
suitable for the recreation of men, and for yielding them pleasure, music is either the first, or
one of the chief, and we must esteem it a gift
of God bestowed for that end. . . . There is
scarcely anything in this world which can more
powerfully turn or bend hither and thither the
manner of men, as Plato has wisely remarked.
And, in fact, we experimentally feel that it
has secret and incredible power over our hearts
to move them one way or other.   Therefore we
ought to be so much the more careful to regu-
late it in such a manner that it may be useful to
us and in no way pernicious." (Calvin, " Preface
to Psalter," 1543).   These words by one so
maligned—I have heard him called, "Such a
wretch as John Calvin "—exhibit the softening
influence of music upon a susceptible if rugged
nature ; and what rugged nature will not be
susceptible who once knows the grace of God
as John Calvin knew it ?   But they lead me to
say, first of all, assuming that you somewhat
experience that which an eminent living preacher
has said, " When you listen to fine music you
hear your mother-tongue," then I say to you,
personally, a gracious life should be a musical

life, melodious and harmonious, that is, flowing, continuous, sweet, rhythmical, consistent, symmetrical, according to Charles Kingsley's injunction to the child, let life be "one grand, sweet song;" or as a greater than Kingsley said, "Make melody in your hearts to the Lord," not only, I take it, in the "psalms, and hymns, and spiritual songs," but in all life. "Hallelujah," "Praise ye the Lord," "Sing unto the Lord a new song," is not a direction for the voices only of those concerning whom the Lord says, "They shall show forth My praise," but concerning the life. And life is not to be dithyrambic but melodious, a melody being a sweet and orderly rhythmical succession of sounds with proper measurement and proper periods of pause and repose. One eminent musician did indeed contend that *melody* simply means a succession of sounds, regardless of sweetness, honeyedness, or beauty; and *harmony*, sounds combined, regardless also, I believe, of their agreement. And so some persons take the view of life, that it is succession of hours, and days, and years, sweet or not. But when I say let life be the outflow of a heart that is melodious to the Lord, I mean that it should be graciously sweet.

And, further, I would urge that in this same way your preaching should be largely musical. I do not mean that you should substitute singing, so-called services of song, for the enforcement of truth by sober, serious preaching. God forbid! Never let sentiment, and the working upon feeling, take the place of earnest dealing with men's understandings and consciences. But I mean, let your preaching have musical qualities in it, rhythm, flow, sweetness, winningness. That which Dr. George Macdonald [1] has said about the poet is only in lesser degree pertinent to the preacher.

" I begin with that which first in the nature of things ought to be demanded of a poet [say also of a preacher,] [1] namely, Truth, Revelation. . . . But let me speak first of that which first in time or in order of appearance we demand of a poet, namely, music. For inasmuch as sense [and preaching] is for the ear, not for the eye, we demand a good hearing first. Let no one undervalue it. The heart of poetry is indeed truth [and so of preaching] but its garments are music, and the garments come first in the process of revelation. The music of a poem is

[1] George Macdonald, "England's Antiphon."

its meaning in sound as distinguished from word," etc. ; and an eminent minister and writer who in early life cultivated music, wrote to me that he had been compelled to abandon that, in order to study how to get as much music into his sentences as possible.

I am not at all unmindful of the whole-hearted absorption which is at once the obligation, the honour, and the privilege and delight of those who would be "able ministers of the New Covenant," and who would be both "pastors and teachers," and also "do the work of evangelists." Sad indeed do I think it that those who profess to have received the Divine call to this gloriously absorbing work should suffer their mental and spiritual energies to be diverted and frittered away by the many petty things which, nowadays, are either thrust upon or dabbled in by ministers of the Gospel. I should say, with Dryden :

> " Is not the care of souls a load sufficient ?
> Are not your holy stipends paid for this ?
> Were you not bred apart from worldly noise,
> To study souls, their cures and their diseases ?
> The province of the soul is large enough
> To fill up every cranny of your time,
> And leave you much to answer, if one wretch
> Be damn'd by your neglect."

I would not weaken the solemn earnestness
of such an appeal. But there is a broad and a
narrow sense in which a man may be "a man
of one idea." It may be that a man has what
we call a "fad," or a "crank," or a "hobby ; "
that he is, in some way, a monomaniac, or that
he is of very limited knowledge, or contracted
sympathies, or poor culture ; but we do not
associate any such thought with the utterance
of the Psalmist : "One thing have I desired of
the Lord, that will I seek after ; " or with that
of the Apostle : "This one thing I do; forgetting the things which are behind, and reach-
ing forth to those which are before, I press
towards the mark." We feel that such pursuit
as this will call to its aid, and subordinate to its
service and aim, all that is refined and noble,
from whatever source derived : " *Whatsoever*
things are true, honourable, just, pure, lovely,
of good report ; if there be *any* virtue, . . . *any*
praise : " this may surely include things mental,
as well as things moral—art as well as character
—as things to "take account of." Moreover,
any "one thing" that a man makes it his purpose to do well, will be better done if he also
can do something else ; either something of
different, even contrasted character, which will

call into play and develop other faculties of
mind, so as to prevent single-mindedness from
becoming narrow - mindedness, or something
which, by analogy or otherwise, will help to
cast some light upon his main pursuit, and, by
presenting it in a different aspect, illustrate the
method or different methods of its pursuit and
accomplishment. How admirably salutary may
the influence be of any collateral pursuit which
is, in itself, both refining and many-sided, as
music is! Such a pursuit may serve not only
to loosen the bow from too constant tension,
but also to furnish a test, a parallel, a touch-
stone, with regard to his own proper work. I
think that the very contrast of the work itself—
musical work, whether performance, or composition, or analysis—renders such a testing
comparison all the more valuable, with regard
to preaching; more so, by far, than any such
comparison with, for example, lecturing on
scientific or any secular subjects. It is not at
all an infrequent practice, with myself, at all
events, to criticise a musical composition by
comparing it with a novel, for instance; the
subjects with the characters, the development
of those subjects with the involvement, the
entanglements of the plot, and so on: and the

rules of art—all that have to do with symmetry, consistency, contrast, the bearing of one part upon another—are mainly the same, whatever the nature of the art. Possibly you may hardly realize or know how much a musical work is one of plan, structure, as well as of impulse and feeling—emotion. But it is so; as much a matter of logical and rhetorical arrangement as any of your sermons.

It is, perhaps, not uncommonly supposed that a musical composer—at all events, if a genius— is a spontaneously emotional or emotionally spontaneous producer of beautiful ideas, which come unbidden, ready-made, in the form in which they are presented to our hearing, rather than the logical, structural, rhetorical setter- forth of pure and applied or developed thoughts. But music, on the contrary, is pre-eminently the art in which, without pre-existing material, a genius who has been defined as "one who kindles his own fire"—first conceives his germ thought—and then works it consistently, co- herently, presenting it in its various aspects— logically, structurally, rhetorically—without mo- notony or tautology, and still leaves the im- pression of a reserve of power. In other words, a musician first produces his own text, not finds it in a treasure-book, as you do yours ; and then proves its suggestiveness, and exhibits its wealth of meaning by the developing processes which the art itself furnishes. I have said that music is pre-eminently the art in which this can be done, and that the musical composer does this —of course I mean the ideal musician. I cannot answer for the musician, but I can answer for the art, and can illustrate and make good my contention. Of Dr. Chalmers, a prince among your order of workers and thinkers, it has been said that he had peculiarly the capacity and habit of taking an initial thought ; and in order to impress it on the minds, and if possible the hearts, of his hearers, reiterating that one thought, not in the same words, or the same form, or mode of presentation, but over and over again, in such differing fashion, that while it was not "in the meantime" (as the Scotch say) recognized as the same thought, and there was no sense of tautology, of monotony, of *paucity* of thought, only of *unity* of thought— a very different thing—the ultimate issue was that that thought had fixed itself in the minds of those who had attended, the fact that they had been hearing the same thing all the while only being discovered on reflection, by finding, experiencing, the hold on the mind which it had obtained. A different process, this, from de-ducing the lessons from the thought, or even from stating its evidences; the first process often being an ingenious method of dissipating, instead of concentrating, the impression, and the latter often being an exercise which may exhibit weak points, and, at best, only convince the understanding, without taking possession of the whole man.

Now music affords, I will hardly say unique, but uniquely multifarious opportunities of ac-complishing this very object, of thoroughly working an idea in such diversified methods, as to interest the hearer, and to illustrate and impress that idea, and show its resources, its suggestiveness, its power, its contents. Let me try to make this audibly plain to you, premising, however, that I cannot undertake to illustrate how you can apply all this in your work. It must be left with your own suggestive rumina-tions, merely showing, as I. quite believe you more or less realize, that there are other ways of treating a subject than firstly, secondly, thirdly, and a few practical suggestions, and so on. In life we are bidden to "adorn the doctrine of God our Saviour;" that is, if not exactly to

decorate it, yet to present it in attractive guise.
And so, in preaching, there are ways of putting
things which are bare, rugged, if not harsh,
repellent. The sovereignty of God, and other
doctrines, which are commonly spoken of, rightly
or wrongly, as belonging to the Calvinistic
system—as though Calvin originated, instead of
logically deducing them—may be so presented
as to appear as barriers in the way of the
salvation of some, instead of as reasons for
adoring gratitude that any are saved ; and justi-
fication by faith may be so presented as to
appear simply as a plan for letting the guilty
go unpunished, by a kind of legal fiction, instead
of the method by which a life is entered upon
of newness of spirit, and loving holiness, in the
place of legal bondage.

But to return to the resources of music. A
given musical theme, either attractive, or comparatively barren of interest, taken alone, may
be so clothed with *harmony*, and so varied
in harmonic presentation, as to change aspect,
and acquire new beauty and power. And it
may be so presented *contrapuntally*, as to be
either the basis, or the prominent part, or a
subordinate part. And it may be so worked,
developed, as to be reasoned out, and shown

as, so to speak, a living truth, with various bearings.

I have used the term contrapuntally, which I may as well at once explain. In old times the melody, or plain-song, in ecclesiastical chants, was taken by the *tenor* voice—that which *held on* (*teneo*, I hold) the melody—as being the piercing voice of men. When boys were introduced, they sang the *altus* (alto), or high part, either the same tune as the tenors, an octave higher, or an independent part. This part, being a melody against another melody, was regarded as *punctum contra punctum*, point against point, from the notes having been called *points*. The bass might also have a part *under* the chief, original melody, leaving that melody as the middle part, and so on. Ultimately the chief melody might be given to the highest voice, that of the women. So that counterpoint was the art of adding one or more parts to a given part, melody, or subject; or, as it has also been defined, " the art of combining melodies." For, whereas that which is now commonly called the *melody* is the highest part, and the other parts, under it, are subordinate supports to it, contrapuntal writing, as distinguished from mere harmonizing, aims, as its ideal, at rendering each of the parts—highest, lowest, or middle—melodious and interesting; or, taking another view of it, as I have said, it treats a subject, a theme, in various ways, in different aspects; showing its power, vitality, virility, suggestiveness. It is not ornamentation or embellishment to hide the bareness, or disguise the paucity, of a theme, any more than when you discourse on the truth expressed in a text, you are doing so because of the poverty or weakness of the truth. You try to bring out its wealth of meaning, so as to bring it home, with all its diversified applications, to the understandings of your hearers. The most perfect exemplification, musically, of this kind of development is the *fugue* form. "Fugues!" you say; "why, are they not dry, unmelodious compositions, scientific, and all that sort of thing, but without any *tune* in them?" Well, gentlemen, you especially had better not say anything about dryness, for it is precisely the charge that people bring against sermons, shallow people, with no earnestness, who only go to church as a religious pastime: and so with people who only regard music as an amusement. Your business is at once to enlist the interest and sympathy of your hearers. You announce your text, and the curiosity, the

interest of your hearers is, for a minute at all
events, awakened, and while they are asking
mentally, " What does that mean? What will
he make of it?" or, if they are a little ex-
perienced, are rapidly drawing up an outline
of what you ought to say about it, you say
something which, according to the rules of *my*
art, at all events, ought to be germane to it,
and so bring them into touch both with yourself
and with the truth which you desire to expound
and to enforce.

Just so with a composer and his fugue. First
of all a short theme or musical phrase, concise,
complete in itself, self-contained, that is, interesting, or at least suggestive, arousing to the
curiosity, is announced by one part. That is the
musician's text, which, please observe, he has not
to *select*, but to *make ;* it is his own thought or
inspiration. An old book, giving directions to
students for fugue-writing, says : "First *choose*
your subject." "Aye! there's the rub." As a
general rule it has to be originated ; and it may
be so poor as not to be susceptible of interesting
working, even as preachers sometimes take as
texts phrases which are, indeed, to be found
in the Book, but which never should be
taken under the pretence of being the founda-

tion of a sermon, enunciating no truth. But, once a musician has a theme, a subject, let me briefly illustrate how he goes to work to treat it.

Each part having one entry of the subject or answer, constitutes that which is termed the *exposition* of the fugue, and there then follows the development of the material therein set forth ; the subject, counter-subject, and auxiliary counterpoints. And with regard to that development, a splendidly rigid rule of consistency and cogency holds, viz., that nothing may be introduced which has not been, in its germ, announced in the exposition ; nothing irrelevant. There will be episodes, indeed, in which, so to speak, the full working is eased a little; but these must be constructed from some portion of the principal or auxiliary themes in the exposition. Who shall say then that a musician, if a fugue-writer, at least, is not bound to be logical and coherent ? Is there any stricter rule that binds even sermon-makers than this, which insists on the avoidance of all non-pertinent digressions, and on keeping to the point or points at issue ?

In all this I have exhibited the musician to you in the logical aspect, as the constructor, with plan, design, and so forth. It will hardly be necessary, nor would it be practicable in

limited time, to go on and illustrate the
rhetorical principles which are brought to bear
on musical compositions. In fugue it is a
stringent rule that the same passage must not
occur twice in the same form; there must be
some difference in the setting, the combination,
the mode of presentation. In fact, musical
composition does very much consider and pro-
vide for, affords, that is, abundant means of
providing for, the different effects to be produced by the ways of putting things.

And is not that an art very desirable to have
at command in preaching, as, indeed, in other
deliverances, even in common talk?

The musical student is warned against modulating into the same key twice in the same
movement; against remaining long in a key re-
mote from the original key in which he started,
if, indeed, he go into such key at all, which
should only be for very special effects. These,
and such rules or principles as these, which are,
in the main, adhered to in the works of all the
great masters, may serve to show that music is
logical as well as imaginative; that reason and
thought are brought into play by her, as well as
emotion and feeling; that a musician does not
meander on in a dreamy or irregular manner,

without purpose and plan, any more than a
reasonable man will stand up to preach with, as
he says, his heart so full that he needs no
previous thought or preparation. We all know
a little of what that comes to in the long run.

Every legitimate calling in life may be made
a means of serving God, carrying out His plan
and order in the world. As Dr. Dale has
somewhere said : " It is part of God's order
that men shall live by eating bread ; therefore a
baker who conscientiously makes good, whole-
some bread is serving Him. It is part of God's
order that we protect our bodies from the
weather by wearing clothes, that we live in
houses ; and therefore a conscientious shoe-
maker or builder serves God." In like manner
I venture to say that it is part of God's order
that the mind, the intellect, the perception of
beauty, the artistic faculties or susceptibilities
with which He has endowed us shall be informed, directed, cultivated, quickened, and
furnished with material upon which to exercise
themselves. If it is " not good that the soul be
without knowledge," neither is it good that the
faculties of appreciation, in the midst of the
world, the universe of beauty in which we are
placed, be left uncultured, unprovided for.

Therefore, every artistic producer and every artistic educator may, in his sphere, serve God : may help to lift his fellows out of dull grossness, making it all the difference to them that they shall go through the world with eyes instead of no eyes ; ears, instead of no ears ; quickened perceptions, refined tastes, instead of stolid materialism, if not sensuality. And I may be pardoned even if I over-estimate my own calling, my own department of artistic culture, in thinking that music has a refining influence, specially delicate, and specially unliable to depraving associations or applications, though fallen man may himself curse any blessing ; and, therefore, I think that in endeavouring to inculcate sound, refined, and noble views about my beautiful art, in my calling as a professor, I may truly, though humbly and imperfectly serve God.

But, gentlemen, friends, brethren, I magnify *your* office, if God has counted you faithful, putting you into the ministry to preach that Gospel which is to be far more than a refining agent, which is to do far more than help and cultivate men, according to the present order ; which is to be a redeeming power, the " power of God unto salvation." You serve Christ the

Lord in a higher plane of service. You know that there was a glorious time when "the morning stars sang together, and all the sons of God shouted for joy,"[1] and that was music indeed! There seemed reason enough for the glorious antiphon and the exultant shout; for was not everything "very good"? But, had they foreseen the discord which was to interrupt the Divine order, the entrance of sin, and sorrow, and death, their joy might have been turned into mourning, and their shout into wailing, when even God Himself repented that He had made man upon the earth and it grieved Him at His heart.

But you also know that in the course of the ages there was again a plan of joy and praise, when

> "The shepherds on the lawn,
> Or e'er the point of dawn,
>   Sat simply chatting in a rustic row;
>     *     *     *     *     *
> When such music sweet
> Their hearts and ears did greet,
>   As never was by mortal finger stroke,
> Divinely-warbled voice
> Answering the stringed noise,
>   As all their souls in blissful rapture took:

---

[1] Job, xxxviii. 7.

The air such pleasure loath to lose,
With thousand echoes still prolongs each heavenly close.

    \*      \*      \*      \*      \*      \*

Such music (as 'tis said)
Before was never made,
  But when of old the sons of morning sung,
While the Creator great
His constellations set,
  And the well-balanced world on hinges hung,
And cast the dark foundations deep,       ,
And bid the welt'ring waves their oozy channel keep." [1]

That was the ushering in of the new creation, of the advent of Him who is " the beginning of the Creation of God," who declares, " Behold! I make all things new."

And once again you look forward through the ages, and the ears of your faith catch the sound of " a new song, . . . ten thousand times ten thousand, and thousands of thousands ; saying with a great voice, Worthy is the Lamb that hath been slain to receive the power, and riches, and wisdom, and might, and honour, and glory, and blessing." [2]

"Why do they sing ? It is because speech is too weak to tell what they feel. Words are the feeblest language of the soul. How poor an

[1] Milton's " Ode on Morning of Christ's Nativity."
[2] Rev. v. 9, 12 (R.V.).

instrument is speech for the great multitude who never acquire any real mastery over it, and who feel it rather a bar against which the tide of feeling breaks, than a channel for the full river of emotion to flow in. Each of us has felt in trying to put into words our grief, our gratitude and love, that we have not been able to tell the half. If this is felt on earth, how much more is it felt in the deeper hearts of heaven, and is it wonderful that they try to utter themselves in praise? 'Worthy is the Lamb that was slain,' they sing, because He has redeemed them to God by His blood?"[1]

This is a testimony concerning the emotional power and adaptability of music.

And that "multitude which no man can number" is even now being made up; "the redeemed of the Lord" are even now returning and coming to Zion with songs and everlasting joy upon their heads: "they shall obtain joy and gladness, and sorrow and sighing shall flee away." And, brethren, one blessed part of your work is to be to teach and help these pilgrims to sing these songs of Zion, so that the "new song" in the heavenly Jerusalem shall not be

---

[1] W. Robertson Nicoll, "The Lamb of God."

a wholly unrehearsed canticle. The fuller your unfolding of the reasons for an abounding joy, by exhibiting to them "the unsearchable riches of Christ," the more consistently by life, demeanour, and testimony you can say to them "Rejoice in the Lord alway, praise is comely for the upright, be glad ye righteous ; again I say, rejoice," teaching them even songs in the night, the more truly will you be the bearers of the heavenly music to their souls, leading them exultingly to exclaim, "Blessed is the people that know the joyful sound ; they shall walk all day in the light of Thy countenance."

But however faithfully you either proclaim the terrors of the Lord, or blow the Gospel trumpet, you will alike be liable to the strangely anomalous experience, at once depressing and dangerous, which was declared to a faithful prophet of old: "The children of thy people talk of thee by the walls and in the doors of the houses, and speak one to another, every one to his brother, saying, Come, I pray you, and hear what is the word that cometh forth from the Lord. And they come unto thee as the people cometh, and they sit before thee as my people, and they hear thy words . . . and, lo, thou art unto them as a very lovely song of one that hath a pleasant voice, and can play well on an instrument: for they hear thy words, but they do them not."[1]  Just an experience of many a player or singer; a gaping crowd listen and applaud, but never take in the refining and ennobling influence of fine music.  But here is depicted the career and experience of many a popular preacher.  The lesson seems to be, neither be satisfied with good congregations, a seeming attention, being in everyone's mouth, everywhere receiving plaudits—a great temptation; nor, on the other hand, be unduly depressed, as though some strange thing had happened to you if no other results seem to follow.  It does not follow that you are unfaithful or unqualified any more than Ezekiel was, who declared the whole counsel of God, whether men would hear or whether they would forbear.

I have endeavoured to elevate your conceptions of music as an emanation from the Divine Mind, a glimpse of the beauty which centres in Him who is the Father of Spirits and the Creator of this beautiful world and universe. I have illustrated its logical and intellectual

---

[1] Ezek. xxxiii. 30-32.

character, as well as its emotional and imaginative aspects, and shown it to be a pursuit, not
merely a pastime ; and as running parallel with
preaching and other mental exercises, with
sermons as well as other structures, have used it
analogically and comparatively, both as a test
and as a help ; may I say also, as a bond of
union between you and me, let us set life to
music, the music of a heart melodious to the
Lord, and, like the prophet, send to that "Chief
Musician " a gratefully and trustfully melodious
heart, at once our fears, our work, and our
hopes ?

The prophet Habakkuk's experience and
outlook were none of the brightest, apart from
the faith by which he lived, and which prompted
him to write his ode—far from cheerful through-
out—and then to send it "to his chief musician
upon stringed instruments." Be yours, brethren,
that faith, and hope, and joy : yours and mine.

# IV

# THE DEVELOPMENT OF MOVE-MENT STRUCTURE

I ESTEEM it a great honour and privilege to be asked to address you on a few successive after-noons on the growth of musical structure and movement writing, for that is the subject that I have undertaken to trace and expound, to the best of my ability, in your hearing. I may as well at once say that I purpose dealing mainly with INSTRUMENTAL MUSIC, though reference may have to be made, now and again, to vocal structure. I have to illustrate the evolution of music left to itself, so to speak, rather than music allied with, and more or less influenced, if not dominated, by alliance with, and some subordination to words and drama. In other words I am to examine the development of that which is nowadays spoken of as *absolute music;* though, in thus narrowing my survey — a sufficiently broad one, however — I do not for one moment intend any reflection on, or dis-

paragement of any contentions in favour of
applied or allied music, of a poetic basis for
music, of the so-termed *Romantic* element, or,
if you will, *Romantic School*, of music. In the
main my subject is technical, which is surely an
appropriate limitation, if it be so deemed, while
addressing those who are studying music as a
craft, however fitting it might be, were I addressing an audience of *dilettanti*, to enlarge
on the æsthetic and other aspects of music.
But this disclaimer is not a dissuasive ; far, very
far from it. Nor, on the other hand, must it be
understood as implying any avowal that the
technical part of music is outside of, or dis-
sociated from, the artistic, æsthetic, or poetical.
This is a charge sometimes implied, if not
expressed, when form, plan, design, are advo-
cated or analyzed ; the nickname "*formalism*"
is used, reproachfully. But if sometimes mere
technical composition is called " music-making "
—and I remember a pupil in this very Institution who used to come to me saying, " I have
made another tune "—let it be remembered that
by the Greeks the poet was termed a *maker ;*
and the word translated *workmanship* is the
word for poem. There is mere mechanical workmanship, and there is artistic workmanship.

G

But, as I said, in studying structure with you, I
by no means dissuade you from giving your
imagination free play, whether in the interpretation of the beautiful music that you hear, or in
the composition of music. Let " mind and soul,
according well . . . . make one music."

I shall have to trace the history of certain
forms or structures; and this will be a section
of the history both of the art which we love,
and of the progressive working of men's minds;
both, surely, fascinating departments of historical
and artistic study.

If I were in search of a poetical motto for
my short course of lectures, it might seem that
the laureate's dictum, " The old order changeth,"
would fitly summarize the whole period which
our review will comprehend, and form the
" moral," so to speak, of our survey. But it is
not so entirely; for, if it were, my very title would
be a mistake. If I am to speak of development, that means unfolding, and unfolding is
not changing in any revolutionary sense. The
term now in vogue is " evolution," and that,
again, implies no cataclysm, no violent change
of method, but such a change as is implied by
growth, enlargement, increased resources, carrying out to fuller issues; this is the kind of

development which we shall have occasion to observe and trace.

The period for our consideration is that which dates from that great change, which, in fact, constituted a revolution in the state of music ; that which has been already described to you as the TRANSITION PERIOD ; a change of tonality, involving also a change in the harmonic system. This was signalized by the recognition of essential discords the Dominant 7th, in the first instance ; and, likewise, by the introduction of the perpendicular method of reckoning and writing music, as contrasted with the horizontal ; in other words, by the *harmonic-progression* system—chords and their context—as distinguished from the *contrapuntal* system of a theme with its adjuncts, satellites, or accompanying parts : to be still further developed into the working of subjects, instead of the accompanying of *canti fermi*. More about this later on.

But it must not be supposed for a moment that this revolution brought about an abandonment of all that appertained to the contrapuntal style ; that the contrapuntal method of treating a theme was discarded in favour of the harmonizing method. That would, indeed, have been a disaster, robbing music of one of its elements of strength. But such a result of the new way of looking at music was no more possible than would be the instant and entire change in the manners and customs of a people through a revolution in government. That which did take place was just that which might have been expected—(I do not think this is being wise after the event)—a gradual assimilation of the two methods, the survival of the fittest of the essential features of counterpoint—of which more almost immediately—and the adaptation of the old method to the new theory, the new light, the new system. I have termed this a gradual process; for, indeed, it has been, in a sense, going on ever since, and is still working, still in progress, although this fact is not always borne in mind, and the non-recognition of it has led to much misunderstanding and much needless controversy among musicians to this very day. Just in proportion as the contrapuntal element, rightly understood, is present in music, assuming it to be otherwise good, in that proportion has it structural power and solidity. And this, as will perpetually be evident, is true even in music that, at first sight, and to the superficial observer, might seem to make no contrapuntal pretensions ; and, indeed, does not, perhaps, make any preten- sions, but neverthless reveals at every step the mastery which comes from contrapuntal train- ing, and the understanding of the true contra- puntal spirit.

For what is the spirit, the essence, of counter- point and contrapuntal working ? Not, em- phatically be it declared, the mere observance of any code of laws, however good, whether rigid or free, severe or lax : not this, though this is how it seems to be presented to students' minds, and to be accepted or resented, for that is hardly too strong a word to indicate the manner of its rejection, ofttimes—by composers. Counterpoint, properly viewed, is not a series of prohibitive or of directive rules ; but ultim- ately amounts to this : the art of treating musical themes or subjects in varied manners, and of putting the subject in the lowest, the highest, or an inner part. Now this is so important— nay, so indispensable a feature in all develop- ment—that, quite irrespective of *strict* or *free*, it must form part of the training of all who aspire to be strong composers ; it must and does so inevitably enter into all structural music, that it cannot be abrogated. The illustrations of this will so repeatedly come up in our afternoons together, that I shall not enlarge on the matter now, especially as my province is not at all controversial, but educational, historical, and analytical. I only repeat my original statement that the new era inaugurated at the transition period was not a termination of the contrapuntal method which had exclusively prevailed, but a carrying it on in union with new theoretical views, absorbing its essential spirit, but enlarging its scope, adapting it to new conditions, which, however, has been done all too slowly. But, be that as it may, the point which I wish to impress upon you is that the emergence, at the transition period, was not from contrapuntal power, but from certain contrapuntal restrictions appertaining to the tonality which prevailed during the contrapuntal school period. And that, whereas in a sense the contrapuntal method of that school was empirical—I say this in no depreciatory spirit or sense, for it was inevitable that empiricism should characterize it—on account of its non-harmonic basis, the contrapuntal habit of thought survived, enlarged by the further understanding of the chord system as it was gradually formulated. So that our system

has not superseded or displaced the contrapuntal, but has established and widened it.
Our modern music is the product of an amalgam
of the contrapuntal and the chord systems.
There was no period at which it was enacted
that, henceforth, there should be no more
counterpoint, and that the chord system should
be the basis of musical composition. Nor was
there, by any means, any abandonment of the
*strict style;* up to this day, as you know, *strict
counterpoint* is still insisted on by some musicians,
as though it were the only counterpoint.

Now turn to another matter, issuing from the
change of view and usage with regard to tonality,
at the transition period ; that, namely, of key-
relationship and modulation, as we now understand it. Once accept the chord of the Dominant
7th, and we, who know something of its power
in determining the key, for the time being, can
perceive that it was but a step further to find
out how readily it lent itself to the making a
change of key, a change of tonic, in the course
of a movement. I am not speaking now of the
old sense of the term modulation, " conceded "
and otherwise. You and I are, happily, living in
*post-transition* times, and I am using terms in
their modern sense. The system of conjunct

and disjunct tetrachords suggested, and instinct, in conjunction with the Dominant 7th, coincided in the suggestion of certain keys as most obvious and natural to modulate to ; and the harmonic series served to justify, within certain limits, this selection of keys.  The *Dominant* to any given note being the first note harmonically produced, after the duplication of the fundamental note, justifies the all but universal choice of the key of the *dominant* as the first key to modulate to from any given major key.  And, obviously, as any key is the *dominant* to another key, which is its *sub-dominant*, modulation to the *sub-dominant* is similarly natural ; being just the reverse process to modulation into the *dominant*, the return journey, as it were.

With regard to the other modulations with which we are familiar, as included in what are grouped as *natural* modulations, those, namely, to the so-termed *relative minor* keys of the *tonic, dominant*, and *sub-dominant*, the explanation seems derivable from another source than the harmonic basis.  Professor Sir George Macfarren contends that " it is a remnant indeed of the Church theory [that is, of the system of ecclesiastical modes] to regard the major mode and its relative minor mode as modifications of the same scale ; "[1] and he characterizes this theory as "opposed to natural truth," and as having " consequently sometimes induced harmonic obscurity in compositions even of the greatest masters : " and he proceeds to argue this point. It is not for me now to discuss this disputed matter ; but merely to record the fact that these so-termed, rightly or wrongly termed, relative minor scales, whether as a remanet of the older system of the modes or not, are those which have been alone selected, whether by instinct, or on principle, or by tradition from of old, as natural to modulate to, from any given major key. Professor Macfarren speaks of the term relative, so applied, as "a stumbling-block in the way of learners ; " and Sterndale Bennett, who was no partisan of Macfarren's theoretical views, said to me, " One can never persuade students that A minor is relative to C major : C minor is its true relative." Now, you are all students : you can judge about the "stumbling-block" matter from experience. I say no more on the subject : I simply point to the facts.

Modulation, then,—the delightful relief of a

---

[1] "Six Lectures on Harmony," p. 25.

temporary change of tonic, like a change of scene, of surroundings, of sensations, often like a ray of sunshine, affording such opportunity for variety and for design in structure, as will be illustrated by-and-by—this was a new factor, so to speak, in the manner of construction of musical movements, with the advent and development of the tonal system inaugurated at the transition period.

And it will be obvious to you that the introduction and recognition of equal temperament is closely allied with this matter of modulation ; and, in its progressive acceptance and comprehension, opened up, also, that method of modulation which is known as *enharmonic*, thus greatly extending the boundaries of key-connection, or at least of progression from key to key; a great gain, certainly, to our modern music, though also liable to become a great snare, as there will be opportunities of showing during our illustrations.

These features of the *transition* and *post-transition* periods, respectively, constitute some of the factors in the evolution and growth of our modern, extended, structural music, especially instrumental music ; and by structural, I mean movements extending beyond a single rhythmical

theme, with harmony; movements with either
contrapuntal and imitational development, such
as the canon and the fugue, or with contrasted or
combined subjects, in different keys, connected
and worked, as in the sonata forms with which
we are familiar.

But, to begin at the beginning, or at least so
near as I may without detaining you in the
region of ancient history, I must again dis-
possess your mind of the idea that there is one
clearly-marked dividing line between the old
and the new, so that no characteristics of the
one appear in the other. Only, in this connection, instead of assuring you that the new amal-
gamated much of the old, I have, on the other
hand, to say that the old did anticipate the new,
to some extent. The fact is that nature re-
sponds to her own laws; the instinct of that
which is artistic in human nature, in the human
mind, coincides with the laws of truth and
beauty. And in certain simple instrumental
music of the pre-transition period there are
beautiful examples of the non-contrapuntal
chord structure, of just what we understand by
harmonized melodies; and these examples, we
may be proud to know, are to be found in the
writings of English musicians. It has been

claimed, indeed, that the founder of instrumental music was *Jan Pieterszoon Sweelinck*, a famous Dutch organist, born in 1562, died 1621 ; who, besides publishing a quantity of vocal music, canons, church music, etc., wrote organ pieces, of which it is said that they " present the first known example of an independent use of the pedal (entrusting it with a real part in a fugue), if not with the first example of a completely developed organ-fugue" (Grove's "Dictionary").

But apart from the fact that there are instrumental works extant by an Italian of the same period, no less a man than the famous *Gregorio Allegri*, composer of the renowned " Miserere " (born 1580 or thereabouts, died 1652), who is said to have written the first known quartet for stringed instruments ; apart from this, I say, there are instrumental compositions by our own *William Byrde* (1546-1623), *Dr. John Bull* (1563-1628), *Thomas Morley* (*c.* 1550-1604), *Orlando Gibbons* (1583-1625), which are quite ignored by the German historian, Eitner, who makes this claim for Sweelinck. And these compositions, some of them, are neither contrapuntal nor strongly characterized by the old tonality.

Orlando Gibbons also wrote, amongst other works, nine Fantasies, in three parts, for instruments ; that is, for *viols*, about which instruments more anon. Concerning these, which are very early specimens of *concertante* instrumental music, Professor Sir G. A. Macfarren wrote : [1] " The Fantasies of Orlando Gibbons are most admirable specimens of pure part-writing in the strict contrapuntal style ; the announcement of the several points, and the successive answers and close elaboration of these, the freedom of the melody of each part, and the independence of each other, are the manifest result of great scholastic acquirement, and consequent technical facility. Their form, like that of the madrigals and other vocal compositions of the period, consists of the successive introduction of several points or subjects, each of which is fully developed before the entry of that which succeeds it. The earlier Fantasies in the set are more closely and extensively elaborated, and written in stricter accordance with the Gregorian modes than those towards the close of the collection, which, from their comparatively rhythmical character and greater freedom of modulation, may even be supposed to have been aimed at popular effect. They would, it is true, be little

---

[1] " Popular Music of the Olden Time," p. 470.

congenial to modern ears, but this is because
of the strangeness to us of the crude tonal
system which prevailed at the time, and upon
which they are constructed. The peculiarities
that result from it are the peculiarities of the
age, and were common to all the best writers
of the school in this and every other country.
Judged by the only true standard of criticism—
judged merely as what they were designed to
be—they must be pronounced excellent proofs
of the musical erudition, the ingenious contrivance, and the fluent invention of the composer."

Such music as this, however, does not illustrate, in any way, the power of the metamor-
phosed tonality, and the changes resultant
thereof; but, mainly, the very important power
of *continuity* which the contrapuntal manner of
writing engenders and sustains. And this is a
lesson for all time. We need the rhythmical
divisions, the phrases, the sections, the periods,
marked by the various cadences which modern
tonality suggests ; but without the involvements, entanglements, overlappings, prolonga-
tions, augmentations, and other devices appertaining to the contrapuntal style, music will be
fragmentary, broken up, tiresome from its con-

tinually recurring stops, like lyrical verse as
contrasted with blank verse. We know, for
instance, how tiresome to the ear—mind, I am
not speaking of the moral sense—the listening
is to a chapter of apothegms, such as the book
of Proverbs furnishes, with its perpetual *anti-
theses* between the righteous and the wicked, the
wise and the foolish. It is inevitable, according
to the nature of the case ; but, from a purely aural
and artistic point of view, it is undoubtedly
tiresome. On the other hand, who would wish
that, in literature generally, Coleridge's example
in " The Friend " should be followed, of giving a
sentence of about six pages without a full stop,
as an exercise for the student in continuous,
sustained, prolonged thought ? We need the
combination of the two elements, the terseness,
conciseness, definition of thought, and the flow,
connection, continuity, bearing of one thought
on another, involvement with another. And,
structurally, this is just what seems the natural
working of the union of the two styles ; the
new, with its recognition of an original key, of
key relationships, and of perfect, imperfect, and
interrupted cadences ; and the old, with its
combination of parts and subjects, and its power
and habit of continuity. My dear old master,

Cipriani Potter, once said to me, "What is it that counterpoint teaches you? Rhythm, phrasing." I listened somewhat sceptically, taken aback; but I pondered, and still could come to no other conclusion than that this is just what counterpoint does *not* teach, except, indeed, in well-directed fifth species, in which reiteration of figures, especially in connection or conjunction with sequences, is introduced. Contrapuntal study teaches varied treatment of subjects, detailed progression and inter-relationship of parts, and continuity. Modern harmony study teaches key-relationship, and, in connection therewith, cadences and rhythm. Unite the two, and, so far as structure goes, you have perfection.

It may have struck you or not that, seeing that instrumental music especially is under consideration, the nature of the instruments written for is a matter for consideration; and, surely, it is almost a truism to say so. The capabilities, and development of, and manner of performance on musical instruments, form an important factor in the structure of the music itself written for them. The limits of the instruments have curtailed the composers, inevitably; and, on the other hand, the irrepressible demands of the music have stimulated the contriving powers of manufacturers, as well as the technical studies of performers.

My subject is not the history of instruments, nor of instrumentation ; but a few facts of an illustrative character may well be mentioned in this connection.

The first fact that I will speak of is, that in early times music was written, alternatively, for *voices or instruments ;* apparently with a view to its availableness for social and family performances under varying conditions. So that, for instance, vocal music was announced on the title page to be "apt for voices *and* viols ;" indicating, it would seem, that if there were not vocalists at hand, the music could equally well be played ; so that, as in the case, for instance, of certain of Orlando Gibbons's compositions, they might be performed either as madrigals, or as quartets or quintets for stringed instruments. I suppose that it may also have been intended that, in the event of a large gathering of performers, the music might be performed by the combined forces, vocal and instrumental ; not our notions, however, of madrigal performance. But they seem to have determined that the people should have music, performable in one way or another.

H

Sir John Hawkins's account of the matter is :[1]
"When the practice of singing madrigals began
to decline, and gentlemen and others began to
excel in their performance on the viol, the
musicians of the time conceived the thought of
substituting instrumental music in the place of
vocal; and for this purpose some of the most
excellent masters of that instrument, namely
Dowland, the younger Ferabosco, Coperario,
Jenkins, Dr. Wilson, and many others, betook
themselves to the framing compositions called
*Fantazias*, which were generally in six parts,
answering to the number of viols in a set or chest
. . . and abounded in fugues, little responsive
passages, and all those other elegancies observable in the structure and contrivance of the
madrigal."

Be that as it may, not only would the music
be restricted to the capabilities of the instruments, but also it would, in such cases, be within
the compass and capabilities of voices ; a circum-
stance which may suggest the remark, in passing,
that the more vocal in character instrumental
music is, the better, of course with obvious
qualifications, especially in these times, when

---

[1] Book xv.

the powers of instruments are so much extended. But the naturalness, or if you like the term better, the prettiness of melodic passages is considerably dependent upon their vocal character.

I have quoted the expression " apt for voices and viols," which leads to a few words upon *Viols*, the precursors of our violin and similar stringed instruments. You may fairly be presumed to know that the very word *Viol* is the generic name for the whole family of stringed instruments played with a bow.[1] (I may mention parenthetically, that the *Vielle* is the name of an old instrument of similar shape, played upon, according to some, not by a bow, but by a rosined wheel; the *Rota*, it is also called, identified by some with the instrument known to us as the *Hurdy-gurdy*.) The *viol* was of various kinds, or registers, trebles, tenors, basses; a *Chest of Viols* meaning a complete set, generally two of each kind. The *viol*, of whatever size or kind, had six strings; it was fitted with *frets*, indicating where the strings were to be stopped.

You may well be familiar with the term, in connection with old music, " a Consort of Viols;"

[1] See Engel, however, " The Violin Family," p. 125.

the term *Consort* being used to denote a group of any one class of instruments playing together; viols, oboes, or the like. When two such consorts were mixed, the music was termed " broken music." In the play, " Henry V.," when the king is courting Princess Katherine, who makes havoc of English pronunciation, he makes her the pretty lover's compliment of saying, " Most fair Katherine, . . . . come, your answer in broken music, for thy voice is music, but thy English is broken."

Matthew Lock published (1656) "40 Airs for Viols or Violins" (then superseding viols) entitled " Matthew Lock, his little Consort."

Then, again, I need hardly remind you of the growth of the *keyed instruments*, of which the representative to us is the *Pianoforte;* the culmination, as it were, of the series which included the *Virginals*, the *Spinet*, the *Clavichord*, the *Harpsichord*, and then our beautiful instrument, which itself has undergone such constant improvements ere it reached its present delightful perfection, if such a word may even yet be used. But it may well be remembered what changes in manner of performance, and therefore in passage structure, have taken place as time has gone on. For instance, the passage of the thumb under the fingers, and the reverse process, was not at first practised. In fact, it is stated that, in the earliest known book on keyed instrument performance, the use of the thumb and of the little finger was prohibited! This, however, was as far back as 1571. Scale and arpeggio passages, therefore, were performed between the hands; and, consequently, not by both hands simultaneously. This, of course, restricted the art of passage-writing very much, and, altogether, the structure of music for such instruments: accounting for the way in which various passages in keyed-instrument music of early times are written.

Then, again, the tone of the early instruments to which I have referred was so lacking in duration, having indeed been humorously described by Dr. Burney (I believe) as " a scratch with a sound at the end of it," that there was nothing about it to suggest or encourage that which we know as the *cantabile* style.

I need hardly enlarge on the development of organ music, in consequence of the difference of G and C pedals.

Such considerations as these serve to account for some of the limitations in the instrumental music, especially in the keyed-instrument music of early times; to which one may well add, moreover, such a fact as that mentioned by Mr. Cummings, that, in those early times, violinists only played in the first position. But, reverting to the limitations in harpsichord performance and capabilities, one can only wonder how so large, broad, grand, and difficult a composition was written, even at a somewhat later period, as, for example, Handel's fugue in E minor.

The whole subject may suggest a lesson as to the importance, in music as in other matters, in order to a right estimate and appreciation, of separating in our minds *essentials* from *accidents*, or accessories; the music itself from the mode of its presentation, *effective* (a dangerous word), or otherwise.

Among the earliest uses of purely instrumental music must undoubtedly be classed its application to the dances of the period. And in connection herewith must be mentioned the rhythmical arrangement of the music. The sense of rhythm, of periodical accentuation, seems *indigenous*, shall I say, to human nature. The way in which the child's, or the untutored rustic's head wags, or foot moves, at any such music as the *march*, or any sort of dance, points to this. And the beginning, the earliest form, of our modern *sonata*, was the *Suite*, *i.e.*, the set, or series of movements, mainly in dance measures. The innate sense of accent, which is indicated in the ways that I have mentioned, thus found expression in artistic form.

I suppose that certain of these dance movements, of which the *suite* was made up, were by no means intended or supposed to be actually danced to, any more than were the *minuet*, or the *waltz movements*—*Valses de Salon*—of modern times. It was simply a matter of suggested rhythm, and the element of continuity added thereto. I myself think there is a certain measure of—I will hardly say affectation, especially with regard to the composers individually, many of them being able writers—but of mistaken method of getting an effect of originality or quaintness in the modern prevailing fashion of writing movements in the measure and rhythm of the obsolete dances, inasmuch as the *esprit* associated with them in the days when they were actually extant as dances—the inspiring motive, assuming that dancing is, as it has been termed, "the poetry of motion"—no longer exists. The supposed quaintness is of the nature of a borrowed sentiment.

But there can hardly be a question of the prettiness, the *verve*, the suggestiveness, of some of these old rhythms; and their adaptability to solid, contrapuntal structure and treatment has been abundantly proved.

Another name for the "set" of movements was *Partita*, meaning a complete whole, divided into parts, or, as we say, movements. The term *partita*, or (French) *partie*, was also applied, however, to what we term *Variations* (see Spitta's "Life of Bach," vol. ii., p. 74). One distinction between the *suite* and the *partita* on the one hand, and the modern sonata on the other, was that in the older composition all the movements were in the same key, whereas in the later kind of composition it is usual to change the key of at least one of the movements. I think that I shall be able to show another bond of union and unity, besides sameness of tonality, in some *suites* by-and-by. I may just remark that a recent criticism of a modern *suite* by an Academy lady was mistaken; she was told that it was a pity that she had all the movements in one key, whereas if she essayed to write after the antique pattern, she was, in a manner, bound by the conditions of the early period into which, for the time being, she voluntarily transported herself.

Another name applied to the older sets of movements, or *suites de pièces*, was *Lessons*, which seems to point to a happy combination of means and end. We have, or had, in our "instruction-book" days, *lessons* in order to learn how to play "*pieces;*" later on we had *exercises*—manipulatory—and *studies*, on special matters of technical execution, in order to prepare us for playing sonatas and such works. But, in those simple days, when they seem hardly to have thought of learning to do something in order to do something else, but acted on the principle that "the way to do a thing is to do it," they made the *lessons* the things to be done for their own sakes. Handel's harpsichord works were called *Suites de Pièces* or *Lessons*, including fugues, as well as preludes, dance measures, and airs with variations. Whether our modern method of practising technical exercises in order to discipline the fingers be the truest economy of time and labour or not, is a matter that may fairly be discussed. Conditions have changed, difficulties have increased and multiplied, and this has brought about a different course or *curriculum*, perhaps inevitably. Be that as it may, I am telling you of the times when there were no Plaidy's technical exercises ; no Czerny's "Vélocité ;" no Clementi's "Gradus ad Parnassum ;" not even Cramer's beautiful "Studio." Just fancy that! If we add to such a state of things the *absolutely perfect intonation* of the contrapuntal era, we may almost sigh for the "good old times!"

It is, perhaps, hardly necessary to dwell much on one characteristic of suites, partitas, dance measures, and much of the music of that period, namely, the superabundance of ornaments (*agrémens*), the names of which form quite a vocabulary, the understanding of which is quite a study, the remembering of which is quite a feat, and the proper execution of which is quite an accomplishment, if, indeed, it be not quite a lost art. The perplexity is, moreover, greatly increased by the fact that different writers express the same meaning in different ways, and mean different things by the same sign ; so that the study becomes a comparative and historical one. The origin of the whole system lay, I suppose, in the necessity of doing something to prolong the impression of a note, and to impart emphasis, where required, in music to be played on instruments such as the precursors of the pianoforte, not amenable to the varieties of tone producible by gradations of touch by the finger, and possessing little or no sustaining or singing power. When playing this music upon our modern instrument, it seems more appropriate, in a considerable number of cases, to produce the effect, whether of emphasis or of *sostenuto*, by the means familiar to us, varying the pressure or the blow from the finger (*only* from the finger), and to omit the ornament. But, on the other hand, the ornaments are in many cases so interwoven with the form and flow of the passages, that to disregard and omit them altogether would be to uncharacterize the music and deprive it of much of its continuity, so that no rule can be laid down. Personally, I omit many of these *agrémens*, both on principle and for comfort's sake. It is very nice when principle and comfort coincide !

Couperin's system of *agrémens* differs much from that of another distinguished French composer, *Jean Philippe Rameau* (born at Dijon, 1683, died 1764), composer not only of *Pièces de Clavecin*, but also of many operas and ballets, in addition to various theoretical works of great importance at the time, though his theories have not continued to be accepted.

In an old book entitled "A Small Treatise of *Time* and *Cadence* in Dancing, reduced to an easy and exact method, by John Weaver (Dancing Master), Lond., 1706," the author says "that in the general Rule for *Measures and Time* in *Musick*, two sorts of Movements are only made use of, viz., *Common Time*, and *Triple Time*, some . . . quicker . . . some slower . . . A *Measure* of *Quadruple Time* is therefore the same as Two *Measures* of *Common Time*." He goes on to speak of "*Loures* and *Slow Jiggs*, which contain six *crotchets* in a *Measure*; for each *Measure* of a *Loure* or *slow Jigg*, is the same with two *Measures* of *Triple Time*." This has been a matter of some discussion among musicians, but, at all events, I have given you a dancing-master's dictum.

*Domenico Scarlatti* (1683-1757), Naples, son of Alessandro Scarlatti, whom I shall have to mention in another connection, wrote very many pieces for the clavecin, or harpsichord. The most generally known are the "Cat's Fugue," and another fugue in D minor. But there is much interest in many other movements of his, though he neither adopted the dance measures nor wrote sonatas—more properly, partitas.

I have called your attention to the fact that

the movements of the *suite* and *partita* were all in one key; the variety, the relief, had to be sought in the change of *rhythm* and *tempo* or pace, *not* in any difference of structure, so far as order of modulations and cadences is concerned, the movements, in some cases being almost like variations on the same progressions of harmonies; see, for example, the dance movements, after the fugue, in Handel's Fourth Suite in E minor. And as in those in the major key the first part of each movement invariably ends in the dominant, and the second part, up to the return to the original key, makes only the most simple modulations, so those in the minor key end the first part with a *half-close* in the key, or a modulation to the minor key of the dominant, with the final chord major, in *Tierce de Picardie* fashion, thus rendering the repeat easy. There is no relief by any modulation to, or final close in, the relative major key. In our modern times, with long movements, more modulations and varied reliefs undoubtedly are necessary, but these do not excuse or justify the restlessness as regards key, and the uncertainty, indeterminateness, as regards tonality, which characterize so much music of this period, and especially the writings of young composers with any yearnings after originality. A lesson may well be taken by these latter from the older writers, as to the resources of the original key, and the possibility of keeping to it without weariness, for some time at least. "A rover's life for me" is a bad motto for a young composer, though, of course, one does not wish him to adopt the other extreme one, "No place like home."

An incalculable advantage seems to have accrued from this use of dance measures, as well as from the fixed change of tonality, and consequent classification of cadences : the advantage, namely, of the regulation, the initiation, indeed, of rhythm and of phrasing,—as contrasted with the comparatively unrhythmical though finely continuous music of the contrapuntal period. And the influence of this sense of rhythm, so connected with tune, is manifest in the music immediately succeeding that in which the dance element prevailed, notably in the one dance measure which survived from the *suite*,—the *Minuet*, with its metamorphosis, the frolicsome *Scherzo*, of yet later times ; but not only in that notable survival, for the rhythmical spirit, yea, even the *dance* spirit, is patent to observation in the final movements, especially, of the sonatas, quartets, and symphonies, of Haydn, Mozart, Beethoven, and others.

Important, however, as is the sense and indication of rhythm,—one of the first elements of form, analogous to the need, in other matters, of points of repose (a room without corners being said to produce insanity to one solitarily confined therein), and a sentence without full stops being a great demand on the attention, the mental strain, of a reader—there are other elements of structure which have to be taken into account. There are involved, or overlapping, or prolonged, or shortened, or otherwise irregular rhythms. There is, also, modulation, or change of key. There is, also, unity of purpose in connection with variety of subject. There is *descant*, not in the old sense of putting a counterpoint to a subject, merely, but in the wider, more modern, general, extended sense, of which we have an instance in our expression, "descanting" on a subject, in the sense of enlarging on a topic, arguing it out, showing its bearings on other subjects, its relationships, its suggestiveness, etc. And in connection with all this, as a part of it, arising out of it, come all the various devices which are comprehended under the general term " working " or " development" in musical composition, and, according to the various ways in which this is accomplished, carried out, will come the various forms or structures of movements in music.

In these various dance-measures, as you have heard, the main points are rhythmical regularity, phrasing and sectionizing, and simple modulations. Inasmuch as, in the harmonic series of sounds (the harmonic chord, as it is called), the fifth or twelfth, which we term the *dominant*, to the original, fundamental sound, is the first produced after the duplication of that fundamental, or root, it is evidently in conformity with Nature's dictates that the key of the dominant has been, as a matter of instinct, of ease, that which has been modulated to, in the first instance, by movement writers, ever since modulation, as an element of structure, came into vogue. And, inasmuch as to return to the original key from that dominant is to modulate to the sub-dominant of the key so started from, in other words, each key being the *sub-dominant* to its own *dominant*, the sub-dominant is also, evidently, a natural key to modulate to. There is, moreover, obviously, the retention in these natural modulations of the old modal distinction or division (call it what you will), of the *authentic*

and *plagal* modes : and it may not be difficult
to discern some symptoms of a similar way of
regarding relationships in the alleged, though
disputed, relationship of a major key with its
so-termed relative minor, and *vice versâ*. So
that one or other of those relative minors has
usually been taken as the secondary keys to
which to modulate from any given major key ;
and the reversing of this process, if the key
started from is a minor key, needs no explanation.

I said to you that the emergence from the
ecclesiastical or contrapuntal style or school,
though, in a sense, an emancipation from thral-
dom, an enlargement of range and scope, together with the change of tonality, was by no
means a renunciation, or an enfeeblement, or a
loss of resources. The old manner of treatment,
suggested by the contrapuntal method, would
assert itself and find opportunities for development in connection even with dance measures.
Take an example. One of the contrapuntal
devices, growing out of canonic treatment, or
rather, perhaps, I should say, exemplified in its
strictest or most pedantic form in that canonic
treatment,—that of imitation or reiteration of a
phrase or figure, soon allied itself with dance

I

measures, in fragmentary form, and with some freedom as to intervals, as a device for obtaining a certain raillery or winsome jocoseness or archness, not at all unfitting in connection with the pastime of dancing. And, as a still further device, in the second part of *gigues*, especially, that quaint presentation of a subject, or of part thereof, known as *inverse movement*, was adopted.

All this, however, was in the main the working of one principal idea or subject, rhythmical, modulatory, and contrapuntal ; and, in these movements, either the dance-measure on the one hand, or the contrapuntal and imitational treatment on the other, was the inspiring motive. It remained to infuse into these the picturesqueness, the variety and contrast, in conjunction with continuity, which would render a musical movement analogous to a narrative or dramatic work, though, admittedly, the analogy is very imperfect. But, putting it another way, independent music, absolute music, not as the expression of words, nor as the adjunct of dancing, was yearning to assert itself. And, assimilating both the power and continuity of the contrapuntal method, and the clearness and rhythm of the harmonic method and the dance-measure, movements of freer development and greater extension were constructed. The *Sonata*, and *Symphony*, and *Overture* forms, as we understand those terms and forms, were the result.

But this is only a very bald summary of the history of modern movement structure; and, I need hardly say, needs and repays tracing in detail. It has been usual to say, broadly, that the *sonata* is the development of the *suite* and *partita;* and that the *symphony* and *sonata* forms are identical. All this, however, needs some qualification, or, at least, explication. For instance, it is contended by one writer, at least, that the *suite* is to be regarded as the precursor of the *overture* rather than of the *sonata*. And this leads fairly to a brief consideration of the various terms for instrumental music, symphony, overture, concerto, and others. *Sonata*, of course, means simply " sounded ; " *symphony*, " sounded together ; " *concerto*, playing or singing in concert, consort, or agreement ; only, though this be so, and we speak of concerted vocal music, the term *concerto* is never applied to such music ; *overture*, an opening piece, obviously, like the other terms, conveys nothing about structure. So that it becomes simply a matter of record as to how these terms have been applied. Taking *overture*, first of all, it was applied originally to the instrumental music opening, or preceding, an *opera* or an *oratorio*. The early form was not that of a single movement, as is most usual now ; but of a series of movements, in fact of a *suite*, as has been hinted above ; in the French style it consisted usually of a *prelude*, a *fugue*, and a *dance tune*, generally a *minuet* or a *gavotte*. This kind of *overture* is said to have been originated by Jean Baptiste Lully (1633-87). The Italian overture consisted of an *allegro*, a slow movement, and another *allegro*, or resumption of the first. Of the French kind, besides Lully, Purcell and Handel wrote many examples. Handel's harpsichord *suite* in G minor, moreover, furnishes an example of this kind. But then the term *sinfonia* was also used for this kind of *overture*. A modern overture is more after the plan of the first movement of a *symphony*, but with less marked division of parts, and no repeat of the first part. Even this description does not apply to melodramatic overtures, and some others, such as Meyerbeer's " Struensee " and Weber's " Preciosa."

Then turning to the word *concerto*, originally, as we have seen, *consort*, of viols, or of other instruments, the term was originally applied to a series of movements for instruments, which also might include a dance movement or a fugue, or both. Some concertos might have an *obbligato* or prominent part for some one instrument, as the *oboe* (*hautboy*); and from this seems to have grown the later form of *concerto ;* that of a work in (generally) three movements for a solo instrument, accompanied by the band, and with interspersed passages for the band alone, termed *tutti.* But such concertos as those without any such *obbligato*, or solo part, answered, in fact, to our *symphony*, except in the nature and extent of the movements. The modern concerto is somewhat on the plan of a symphony, so far as the structure of the movements is concerned, but on a more extended scale, an epitome, called the first *tutti*, preceding the entry of the solo instrument. Even this form, however, has now wellnigh passed away, so far as composers are concerned, and has given place to a more compressed form, and with the solo instrument more like one of the band—an excellence observable, moreover, in some of Mozart's pianoforte concertos, still more so in those of Beethoven, Mendelssohn, and others.

Then the term *symphony* is, with us, applied to that which is, in fact, a sonata for the orchestra. But here again there has been interchange of terms; for even as the early overtures were also termed *sinfonias*, so some old editions of, for instance, Haydn's *symphonies*, term them, on the title page, *overtures*. This, however, need not confuse us as to the structural matter.

As the use or incorporation of dance-measures in works consisting of series of movements for an instrument was gradually abandoned, the term *sonata* came into vogue. Kuhnau (1667-1722) is said to have been the first to apply the term to a series of movements, and it was adopted by Purcell, Arne, Bach, Handel, and many others, sometimes for a single movement only. The term was used for works for several instruments; but it came to be applied exclusively to works in several movements for one, or at most two instruments, the terms *trio*, *quartet*, etc., being used when more than two were employed, the structure of the movements remaining the same, however.

Now what is that structure ? Let us consider primarily that of the first movement, which is generally called *first movement*, or *sonata*

form. Speaking generally, it is just the enlargement, the extension of such form as that which
in a large number of cases was exemplified in
the first movement of the *suite* or *partita*,
namely, a subject in the primary key of the
piece; a modulation, such as I have already
specified, bringing about a close of the first part
in that new or secondary key; a second part,
consisting of some matter built on, or at least
continuous of, and suggested by that of the first
part, but with some modulation; and then a
return to the original key, and possibly to the
original subject. Of course this is a mere outline sketch of such a movement, for instance, as
the *Allemande;* but it will suffice for comparison, as well as to prompt the question:
Wherein does a sonata movement differ from
this? Is it merely in dimensions?

The answer, first of all, might be that the
sonata movement is free of all rhythmical dance-
measure trammels, though of course the composer may or may not permit suggestions of a
rhythmical character to influence him. Indeed,
in some early sonatas there are, perhaps, symptoms of such influence.

But the further reply has still to be made, in
which you will probably have all along antici-

pated me. The sonata movement has more than one principal or prominent subject, and a special feature in connection with these is that, by contrasted rhythm, the sameness inevitably attaching to the *suite* movements is averted, or at all events avertible; and, in addition to this, opportunity is given for much more extended development. The sameness of which I have spoken is not felt in the briefer movements, neither is the need of development. Such undeveloped movements consisting, it may be said, of one extended subject, or little else, with first and second parts, are nowadays sometimes designated as in *song form* when not in *dance form*. But the sonata movement on the more extended lines that I have briefly sketched, is really an artistic structure, with design, proportion, working, although a recent writer has said that such music, unless with what is termed a "poetic basis," is not a work of art at all—only a luxury!

.

## V

## SOME THOUGHTS CONCERNING
## MUSICAL COMPOSITION[1]

THE announcement of the subject on which I
am to address you is sufficiently general, not to
say vague, to preclude any but the most con-
jectural anticipations on your part as to what I
shall deal with. The vagueness need not extend
beyond the title, however; the generality may
prove to be only for the sake of inclusiveness.
I hope that I shall be definite, not purposeless
or hazy; for I have undertaken to express to
you "thoughts," not notions, or "fads;" nothing
less would be worthy of the attention of thoughtful listeners, such as those composing my present
audience. Moreover, to justify myself in speaking to you at all, in response to your highly
complimentary invitation, I must, though with
diffidence, venture to say that I have been
thoughtful—not merely impressionable—con-

[1] A paper read before the Western Section of the Incor-
porated Society of Musicians, at Bristol in 1893.

cerning the subject which interests us all, ever
since I first tried my hand at serious structural composition, by writing my first pianoforte
sonata not less, I think rather more, than forty-
eight years ago.   Before that time, indeed, I
had in a way composed; but then my thoughts
were wandering thoughts.   At the period, however, to which I have specially referred, I endeavoured to discipline my thoughts without
any counsel, advice, or guidance, either as to
how to do it, or as to the necessity of doing it
at all.   Those were days when people had not,
as we are told they have now, had enough of,
and become tired of, sonatas and sonata form.
Those were days also, in which it had not become the fashion to sneer at Mozart's sonatas,
almost at his symphonies, nay, even at his
operas, and quite to discard his concertos.  At all
events, I, never suspecting in my reverence, that
to study a sonata of Mozart's would retard my
progress, dwarf my aspirations, narrow my perceptions, formalize and stiffen my style, limit my
horizon, did take down a volume of those so-
called third-rate and effete compositions, study
one of them, without any aid but that which its
own straightforward clearness, and transparent
beauty furnished, and, without any knowledge

of such terms as first and second subject, development, free fantasia, or the like, saw the
whole thing at once, in outline at least; and I
knew what sonata-form was.  It was that in G,
and so little versed was I in critical analysis,
that, though I suppose I was acquainted with
the prohibition of consecutive 5ths, I did not
detect those in bars 36, 37, etc.  Then and
there, on that memorable morning to me, I
turned my first composition lesson from Mozart
to practical account by writing the first movement of my first sonata.  I have never wandered
in musical thought from that day to this.  But
I intrude this little autobiographical sketch upon
you to emphasize this truth : not to wander
does not mean not to advance ; to hold fast to
early-imbibed principles does not imply no on-
ward progress, no enlargement.  Knowledge
and understanding must be cumulative, not sup-
planting or usurping ; and knowledge such as
I then gained, though true and unalterable, was
not final or terminal, but stimulating and helpful
for all future observation and study : and—to
return from this personal digression, with many
apologies for the egotism—rendered me, from
that day forward, thoughtful about musical composition ; I was going to say a thoughtful man,

but I was only a boy when the self-initiated
process began; self-initiated, that is, with the
helpful prompting of my kind friend Mozart,
for such he seemed at once to become, letting
me into the secrets of his craft, which I had
longed, oh, how yearningly! to grasp.

Now, as I have been thinking all these years,
on this matter—on the art of musical composition—I have jotted down in my mind, rather
than on paper (though I have done not a little in
that way) thoughts, not random, though sometimes fragmentary, from which I venture to offer
you a very few selections; not very original,
probably, but, in their obviousness, such as may
often have suggested themselves to you; none
the less acceptable to you, it may be, inasmuch
as there is a certain satisfaction in hearing that
others have thought as we ourselves have also
thought, but have not said.

First of all, let me say a word or two on the
subject of originality in musical composition.
In connection with the tendency to which I
have alluded, to discard old forms, and with them
the composers who have adopted them, and to
regard them as formalists, there has been a
manifest spirit of enterprise in striking out new
paths, and endeavouring to express musical

thoughts in new methods, and after new fashions. There is the idea prevalent that the old forms have been carried to such perfection by the older masters—this much is conceded by even the most advanced writers of the present day—that any continuance in those methods must, of necessity, be of the nature of working in a groove or rut, and, perhaps, betray the weakness and inferiority of those who so work; though this latter consideration, if it be implied at all, is only hinted at with diffident reserve, as not proven, and, therefore, not to be urged with any mock humility. However, it is well that this acknowledgment of the perfect achievements of our predecessors should be made; it is well that there should be diffidence as to emulating those achievements; and not unwise to acknowledge that, under the circumstances, it is politic to work in different lines. This brings up such questions as: What is Genius? What is the spirit of the age? How does this spirit manifest itself in works of art? Whether are the men of the age—the prominent great men—the factors or the products of its spirit? Questions, these, which are far too wide for any adequate treatment in such a paper as this, and, indeed, quite beyond its scope, as well as beyond the function or ability of your lecturer to deal with. But a word or two as to their bearing on our subject may be permitted.

I believe that it was Rousseau who said, concerning genius and its definition : " If you have it, you need no explanation of it; if not, no definition can make it intelligible to you," or words to that effect. We call it the Divine fire ; John Foster the essayist termed it the capacity to kindle one's own fire, though we may be sure that he, of all men, did not say that in any atheistic or irreverent sense. But we ordinarily understand by the term, as regards productiveness, the power of producing that which is new in thought, in idea, as distinguished from that of reproducing, with whatever novelty or difference of mode of presentation. There is such a capacity as that of an affinity with genius which can take it up, more or less sympathetically, and so imitate it, with unintentional unconsciousness, as to seem almost like it, almost as good, without plagiarism, especially if associated with scholarship ; and it needs nice perception, and discrimination, and experience, to discern the difference, to distinguish the counterfeit—the honest counterfeit, if the term may be used—from the true. It is partly a matter in which "old birds are not caught with chaff," but not only so. There is much music that cannot, in fairness or in any true sense, be termed " chaff," being thoughtful, refined, scholarly, fascinating, finished, masterful in structure—any or all of these—but yet is not the product of the creative faculty. I have heard it said of a beautiful little landscape picture, " Yes, it is very nice, but it is in a borrowed style ; " and, knowing as I did the artist, and the circumstances and influences under which the picture was produced, I recognized the truth of the criticism. And, to speak of another art, respecting which I pretend to no technical or critical, historical or comparative knowledge, I am told that, for instance, Flaxman and Chantrey, both eminent, differ, *inter alia*, in being, the first a genius, the other a finished and refined artist : and so with our own art. A very excellent composer, now deceased, said to me, I think, as a plea for comparative non-productiveness, " It is of no use writing what others have already written." And there can be no question of the fact that much music that one hears, of recent issue, has been previously written, so far as the essence, the ideas, are concerned ; it is *re*-production, not production at first hand. As

Sterndale Bennett once said to me in effect,
when I asked him whether a certain work, just
produced by an English composer, was good,
"Yes, I think so; but people hear so much
music, that it is in a sense easy to write fairly
hearable music, from reminiscences of current
works, without actual plagiarism." On the
other hand, a popular ballad-writer once said,
when showing me one of his newest popularities,
"It is so difficult to be original nowadays, isn't
it?" To which the reply in my mind, though
I am not sure of having uttered it, was, "It is
not at all difficult, any way; if you have original
ideas, they come; if not, it is a matter of im-
possibility, not of difficulty, to utter them." But
people try to be original, and of course the
result is eccentricity, which is the parody of
originality. The avoidance of commonplace-
ness, or conventionality, is not to be sought by
trying to be uncommon, but by being natural,
according to one's own nature, thought, feeling,
and attainment; and then, if there be anything
original in one, it will develop itself in its own
way. It is in art, as in character and conduct
and manners. In character, the man will seem
most original who most closely imitates the one
immaculate, perfect pattern given to us.

We might fairly return, however, upon the question : After all that has been written, is it possible to write anything original? and if so, wherein will that originality consist or manifest itself? What room is there for it? Have not all chords been discovered, and, on some system, been characterized and classified, and their various progressions been determined? Are there any more worlds to conquer?

Now, it would be curiously interesting to trace, in detail, what might almost be termed the history of genius and originality, and the exploring or developing spirit in music. It has been partly done. We all know about the development of tonality from the tetrachords and the hexachords to our modern scale : the leading-note and the sub-dominant, and the admission and full recognition of the dominant seventh, and so on, to other fundamental discords ; just intonation, mean temperament, and all the rest of it, with the conflicting theories, the frowns of conservative theorists—not to say formalists— at radical innovators and free lances, and the hindering, discouraging spirit with which even explorers, the Columbuses of the art, have been regarded. And the landmarks of such history are, upon the whole, so defined, that one may

K

almost apply to our art, if we changed technical
terms, Scott's *dictum* concerning another art :

> "The towers in different ages rose ;
> Their various architecture shows
> The builders' various hands."

But the details of development might, with
advantage and interest, be still further traced
than hitherto ; one lesson, however, resultant
therefrom, would be that originality has not
begun, or indeed at all been marked by defiant
or sneering contempt of the past, but by reverent
study of its achievements ; and another, analogous to it, that it has been, in most cases, in-
tuitive, not to say unconscious, rather than a
sought-out invention.    Sometimes, indeed, it
has been the outcome of study, speculation,
experiment, rather for the satisfaction of the
inquiring mind of the composer than with any
idea of posing as an originator before the outside world, as in the case of J. S. Bach, notably
in his " Chromatic Fantasia," styled, by Sir G. A.
Macfarren " that extraordinary anticipation of
modern resources, that prophecy of all that is
accomplished in the music of the present, and
all that can be possible in the music of the
future ;" though I am aware that he also says
that "it would be groundless as arrogant to

assume that he employed [the latest discoveries
of modern times] experimentally." Be all this
as it may, however; it remains true that whatever a composer does in the way of advancement, enlargement, novelty, it should still be
felt that, as Wordsworth says :

"The music stirs in him like wind in a tree."

But we have not answered the question,
Wherein does originality consist? and Genius?
Certainly not in ignoring the past, and beginning *de novo;* nor in such matters, merely,
as exceptional combinations or progressions;
though there may, and probably will be, some
of these, with an original thinker. Nor, though
this is more the prevalent notion just now, does
it consist necessarily, or mainly, in the rejection
of old forms and structures, and devising new—
new movement-plans—though some development, in one or other direction, of existing
structures, some diversion from beaten paths
and conventional methods, may very likely
result from that independence of mind which
is a factor or important element in true originality. But Beethoven's early sonatas, for example, though on old models, were not mere
reproductions of Haydn and Mozart; one re-

cognizes that the composer is uttering his own thoughts, giving vent to his own feelings, though in familiar and accepted phraseology. And for many a year did he use that same phraseology, though he may, to carry on the metaphor, if metaphor it be, use longer words, more involved sentences—though not much of these—and more extended paragraphs, and even chapters, as he advances, and feels his power. All along, is it not with him, as with all geniuses, that, as Ruskin says, there is "the evidence of ease on the very front of all the greatest works in existence? Do they not say plainly to us, not 'there has been a great effort here,' but 'there has been a great power here'? It is not the weariness of mortality, but the strength of divinity which we have to recognize in all mighty things," etc. In short, there is a subtle *something* which tells us that a composer is expressing himself *from within;* and then we call that a manifestation of *genius*, as distinguished from expressing himself *well*, which is the result of study and discipline, and we call that *scholarship*—very important and advantageous, doubtless; the lack of it may retard, if not ruin, a genius. This is why, to make a personal reference, I call Dussek a genius, for

which I have more than once or twice been
taken to task by those who perhaps do not
know his best works (for he wrote a heap of
comparative rubbish) ; but when the real Dussek
expresses himself, as in the " Farewell " sonata,
notwithstanding a monotony about the last
movement, brimming over with sentiment as
it is ; or in " L'Invocation " sonata, every subject in which is an effluence of emotion ; or in
the " Elegy on the Death of Prince Louis
Ferdinand," an outburst of grief from a loyal
friend at the loss of a sympathetic companion—
a genuine " In Memoriam "—and in the fantasia
and fugue dedicated to Cramer, though the
fugue is not to be held up as a model of scholarship ; in these, and certain other works ;—then,
I contend if anyone denies genius to Dussek,
such denial leads one to ask wherein there can
be real, healthy, musical sympathy and susceptibility. It is more charitable, however, to
suppose that the unwillingness to concede the
genius to Dussek must arise from non-acquaint-
ance with these fine works, a judgment based
upon acquaintance with only his less individual
works, or a postulate that music written in the
then current forms and idioms could not be
reckoned as the product of genius or originality.

And this last-mentioned presumption reminds
me to say that there can hardly be a greater
mistake than to think that writing in accepted
forms is a conventionalism that betokens a lack
of original genius; or that the possession of
this faculty is at all evidenced by departure from
such conventionalism; that such departure is a
symptom of independence of thought, rather
than of undisciplined thought.    I am not for
one moment contending against any enlargement or variation of accepted plans, or any
excursions into new realms.    But the whole
history of the art of composition bears out the
statement that genius has manifested itself, in
the first instance, in connection with current
methods; and, generally, without indication of
impatient irritation at conventionality, whatever
development may have subsequently ensued.
I am not inclined, moreover, to assent to the
recently expressed pronouncement that the day
of sonatas and sonata-form is passed.    There
is, indeed, a phase of thought, shall I call it? or
feeling? rather, of restlessness, which characterizes the productions of our time, and which is
eminently symptomatic of that which I have
referred to as "the spirit of the age," not in
music alone, but in politics, religion and theology,

philosophy, and other matters. It may be a sign of vitality, and, as such, is to be regarded as much preferable to stagnation, or mere movement in a groove. Sometimes it manifests itself in such wise as rather to indicate indecision, and lack of continuous power or grasp. For instance, as having to do with young aspirants in composition, I may mention the uncertainty as to tonality which is so common in their efforts. I have had placed before me compositions in which, for many bars, not even the composer could determine, not merely the prevailing key, but definitely the key for any one bar. The first half bar might be in E flat, but the second might be in C minor, were it not for a certain note which—so the young writer said—might be considered as a sort of passing note, or a chromatic alteration, leading to—ah! no, though, that would not hold good, because of that chord at the beginning of the next bar, and so on, and so on ; and I have had to be pacified by being pointed on to a double bar, where, undeniably, there was a cadence in some definitely assignable key. And another restless feature, observable in these productions, is indecision and changeableness of time and rhythm ; I do not mean of *pace*, but of time-signature, and the rhythm thereby indicated. There seems often the lack of power to think out an idea in its own congruity, so to speak. This is by no means so infrequent as those not having to teach young composers might suppose.

What genius, however, what self-revelation there may be, or what identification with the sentiment to be expressed, there may be, in some such examples even of indecision or restlessness! To mention one or two. How fascinating—sadly fascinating—as almost a bit of mental autobiography, is the first movement of that exquisite incomplete work, Schubert's unfinished symphony in B minor! with its broken off second subject, telling of unaccomplished possibilities, lack of resolute will-power, and much that renders one regretful in the career of that undisciplined genius!

And then to pass to another emanation of genius, though not in its highest flight, but still charming, the first movement, short, and not in full sonata form, of Sterndale Bennett's almost last work, "The Maid of Orleans," with its changeableness from $\frac{12}{8}$ (four bars) to $\frac{6}{8}$ (two bars) back to $\frac{12}{8}$ (four bars), $\frac{6}{8}$ (one bar), $\frac{12}{8}$, $\frac{9}{8}$, $\frac{12}{8}$, $\frac{9}{8}$, and so on. I take this, certainly not as indicating any lack of definiteness in the mind of

the composer, whose unrevolutionary conserv-
atism some of us remember so well ; but as
an instance of that identification of which I spoke
just now—identification with his subject, or
(might I say) historical imagination ; that which
he is pourtraying being *La Pucelle* " In the
Fields," before she is summoned or constrained
to presence herself " In the Field." While she
is placidly pursuing her pastoral calling, of
which she afterwards sings :

> " In innocence I led my sheep
> Adown the mountain's silent steep,"

there still are (as I interpret it) prophetic
movings within her as to the change which
shall come over her, when, for her country's
sake, she shall sing :

> " The clanging trumpets sound, the chargers rear,
> And the loud war cry thunders in mine ear."

The restless movings seem to me to be indicated by the frequent rhythmical changes or
oscillations, though some might think that the
meanderings and wanderings of her flocks were
rather in the mind of the composer. But, in
any case, there was a purpose, very definite,
in the apparent indefiniteness ; it was no weakness.

The "spirit of the age"—of this age—as I

have said, seems restlessness, experiment, adventure, exploration, inquiry, dissatisfaction with old and accepted conventional methods and conclusions. Often, however, the newer method embodies no new, original idea; is only a disguise of paucity of fresh thought. But people are easily taken in by the more novel manner of presentation, which may be more attractive and glittering than the old; and they mistake it for new, or at least improved thought. Some newer manners of presentation result from advancement in executive skill, extension of its scope in connection, moreover, with improvements in instruments themselves. It is important to cultivate the habit of discerning the essential as distinguished from the accidental; the distinction between the strength, beauty, purity of an idea, and the effectiveness of its setting, the mode of its presentation.

This suggests a few remarks as to the subject of mannerism in composition, as resulting from the spirit of the age at the time, on the one hand, or the individuality of the composer, on the other. Mannerism has to do with mode of presentation of thought, with construction, rather than with thought or idea itself, although the two are not wholly distinct; the nature of the idea must suggest its method of outflow. Or, to state it in another way, the means of expression that are within the reach of a composer must shape, and either narrow or widen, his habit of thought. Though it may be also that ideas may struggle within him which will, when expressed, tend to the extension of existing methods, as in the case of Mendelssohn with the orchestra, and other writers, subsequently. But there is, as I have more than hinted, a mannerism of an age as well as a mannerism of an individual; in music as in literature. In the latter, we should, for instance, easily detect it in the manner differences of, say, the Elizabethan, the Georgian, and the Victorian periods respectively. And this must be kept in mind in listening to music, that we may neither unduly depreciate nor over-praise any music, because of its antique guise or its modern freshness, to whichever manner our own preferences lean.

Some mannerisms are also, to coin a term, narrowisms; as in the case, for instance, of Spohr, with his chromatic and enharmonic progressions. Others are somewhat indicative of idiosyncrasies, habits of thought, or preferences. Two of such mannerisms may be pointed out, in no spirit of depreciation, in Mendelssohn.

One of these is the method of termination, so frequent, almost constant or invariable in his pianoforte music, a sustained note in the melody, with either repeated chords, or arpeggios, underlying it.

The other is in marked contrariety both to the principles of acoustics, the old rules of counterpoint, and the directions that we generally give to harmony students—the fondness for doubling the major third.

When architecture was termed "frozen music" —I know not by whom—I imagine that the fixity and definiteness, rather than coldness, was intended to be indicated; otherwise a reflection upon the architect's art would be implied, which he would hardly be willing to accept. But while music is so emotional and warm and mobile, it must be remembered that it is also an art into which that which Goethe termed "Architectonics" largely enters; the principles of structure, symmetry, proportion. And while not the least antagonism is intended to that which is termed the *Romantic* School, as distinguished by its partisans from the *Classical* School—that is, the emotional as contrasted with the structural—it may be reasonably urged that the latter, if there must be a separation, is that to which, having the elements of permanence, students' attention should first and mainly be directed. It is not meant, in saying this, that emotion is not, in the main, the same in all periods—human nature and feeling, with its fluctuations, being sufficiently uniform to "make the whole world kin"—yet as in the youthful period of studentship emotion is all alive and soon stirred, the corrective, counterbalancing influence of structural music is more profitable and desirable for, and adapted to reward, *study* than that which is more romantic. Music, moreover, if it have the form, need not have the frigidity, which the definition quoted of architecture might be taken to imply.

But let me bring my remarks to a close in a more serene atmosphere than that of even the mildest disputation. If architecture is called "frozen music," what about music itself? Let Carlyle answer the question. " Music is well said to be the speech of angels ; in fact, nothing among the utterances allowed to man is felt to be so Divine. It brings us near to the Infinite ; we look for moments, across the cloudy elements, into the Eternal Sea of Light, when song leads and inspires us."

Yes ! let us endeavour to maintain that high

level of feeling, of aspiration and expectancy, and of desire; only remembering that the blessed hope is not a mere sentiment, but is attached to character, not to mere mental refinement: that the true Hope is part of the great triad of graces; Faith its foundation, Love its fruit; "these three." And then we may rationally and justifiably be led and inspired to sing for joy of heart, and congratulate ourselves that we are devotees of the one beautiful art of whose abiding continuance and perpetuity in the Eternal Light we are assured.

# VI

# COUNTERPOINT IN MODERN
# FREE COMPOSITION[1]

You have done me the honour to invite me to
spend an afternoon with you in musical intercourse, not with the purpose that we should
while away a Saturday half-holiday, but that we
should consider some subject in connection with
our art, with that earnestness which will become
us, as a company of musicians, and become you
—not myself—as attached to the Royal College
of Organists ; and, again, become you as robust
sturdy northerners, who do everything to which
you put your hands or apply your minds with
thorough-going energy and determination ; and,
still further, will become you as musicians, meeting in the county which gave birth to my many
years' friend, William Sterndale Bennett. I have,
with pleasure and pride, accepted your invitation ; pleasure, because I am like-minded with

[1] Delivered before the Royal College of Organists, in
October, 1897.

yourselves, in devotedness and earnestness with
regard to our beautiful art, and that inspires me
with a feeling of fraternal fellowship, in addition
to that of personal friendship with a few whom
I do not meet for the first time; pride, not because I am puffed up with any notion of knowing
more than you do, and, therefore, of being entitled to speak with lofty superiority, or with
pedagogic dogmatism; but that I should be
esteemed worthy and able to endeavour to
stimulate your thoughts, possibly in some direction in which they have not previously moved,
on the subject which I have chosen for my lecture.  " Iron sharpeneth iron ; so a man sharpeneth the countenance of his friend."   That has
been happily termed " the intellectual value of
friendship."   We are all friends because of
music ; the " heavenly maid" with whom we
may all be in love without any jealousy.   But
it needs the sharpest iron that a Londoner can
bring with him, to sharpen the countenances of
Yorkshiremen, or of any northerners.   At all
events, however, we may prove and experience
a little of " the intellectual value of friendship."

Now, please observe the title of this lecture :
" Counterpoint in Free and Modern Composition."  You will notice that I have not said

"Free Counterpoint," nor "Strict Counterpoint." Why I have not used either term or prefix may appear as we proceed. But I have prefixed the designation "free" to Composition; and have associated with it the word "modern."

An eminent writer and lecturer on music, lately deceased, once made a pronouncement in my hearing which I will immediately quote; but, as I shall have to animadvert on it, I will first of all say that for his stores of laboriously and patiently accumulated knowledge concerning music in certain of its departments, notably all that had to do with ancient modes, and the contrapuntal principles, rules, and restrictions therewith associated and exemplified in early church music, and for the thoroughness and clearness with which he was accustomed to set them forth, I entertain the most appreciative respect. We were young associates; he in a Byron collar, I in a jacket; were separated by his change of residence for many years, and then met when both were advanced in years, and had a little intercourse, just for the remnant of his life; but we did not have opportunity for controversy. Well, once, after exhaustively treating of such subjects as those that I have specified, and endeavouring to establish the thesis that, on account

L

of acoustical principles the contrapuntal regu-
lations and procedure which he had illustrated
constituted the basis of true musical art, he
wound up with this pronouncement: "Free
Part-writing you may have in these times; but
Free Counterpoint, never!" I think he went on
to contend that the very term, "Free Counterpoint," embodied an anachronism, a solecism.

Now I think that such a pronouncement
brings us face to face with a misapprehension
which involves the begging of the whole question that has of late years been the subject of
much discussion; and that this misapprehension
has obscured the real point which has been,
or has been thought to be at issue, namely,
what is counterpoint, and what is the object in
studying it? The reply to this question which
would express the notions lurking in many
minds apparently—especially students' minds,
perhaps—would be that counterpoint is the term
for a set of rules as to what they ought not to
do in composition; with a few as to what they
ought to do, these few, however, being usually
very awkward to manage. Of course no one
puts it thus in plain terms; but I believe that
this is not only the notion in the minds of
students, fostered by teachers and books, the

teachers, in not a few cases, having the same distorted, crabbed view lurking in their minds.

Now while, of course, in the learning how to do anything, there must be prohibitive and restrictive, as well as positive and directive rules, the first point, surely, should be, what, after all, is it that is to be done? and why? for what purpose? And the simple answer to this inquiry about counterpoint and contra-puntal study, seems to me to clear the whole atmosphere.

For what is counterpoint? Of course there is the answer ready that it is the adding one or more parts to a given subject. But this hardly differentiates it from harmonizing. There is that which I have elsewhere given, that it is part-writing in its largest, most extended sense. Good again; but by no means covering the ground. There is, further, the favourite one that it is "the art of combining melodies;" it would be nearer the mark to say, "the combining of parts, each of which is melodious;" but I am not sure that this does not convey the idea of some such uncontrapuntal ingenuities as placing the National Anthem as a bass to "Rule Britannia," somewhat as Moscheles has done in "Recollections of Ireland," and such pieces, managing to fit them in somehow, with a little mutual concession. I need not say that such a process is not at all what we understand by counterpoint. I think that a twofold statement, if not exhaustive any more precisely or fully than these others, carries more of what, as a course of study, counterpoint is designed to do. It is (1) the art of adding different kinds of accompaniment to a given subject, as exemplified in the five species; and (2) the art of taking such given subject above, below, or in the midst of such added parts, as exemplified in its fullest, most elaborate way, in fugue. It is thus the training process for *combinational* structure in composition. Movement writing takes in also *successional* structure; how subjects may follow one another, and so on, in such order as to develop and constitute a complete and consistent whole. Now if that which I have just given be not the just statement of the philosophy of counterpoint, I know not what is; and I fail to understand the object of the paraphernalia of a contrapuntal course. Quite aware, as I am, that a definition, to be true to its etymology, should state all the essentials and none of the accidents of the thing defined; and quite acknowledging that, in that sense, I

have not given a definition; I yet do not detect
a flaw in my statement, for a practical purpose.
And if so, I ask confidently, is this a question
of strict or free? Is there any sort of warrant for
such a *dictum* as that which I quoted; that,
while we may have free part-writing, we can
never have free counterpoint? with the most
modern harmonies conceivable, surely there may
be variety of forms in the parts, as in the five
species; and different super-positions of subject
and accompaniments? As I have said, the very
pronouncement involves a *petitio principii;* it
begs the question as to what counterpoint is,
assuming as a premise that the term carries with
it the prefix strict; and then, of course, the conclusion follows. But were it true, it would follow
that Bach's Fugues are not counterpoint; for
assuredly they are not what the books and the
rules enjoin, and call strict, as we may presently
see.

Now at this point I interrupt myself, even as,
and because, you are ready to interrupt me, and
to say to me: "Ah! then; after all, you are a
revolutionist, and are discarding all that yourself
and others have been teaching us about strict
counterpoint, with its rules, fetters, worries, and
all the rest of it; and, orthodox as we have

thought you, are now the advocate of free, as against strict counterpoint."

Nay! I have said nothing to justify any such surprised expostulation. At the outset, I begged you to observe that my title was not either " Free Counterpoint " or " Strict, ancient Counterpoint;" but " Counterpoint in Free and Modern Composition." For, all along, I have had in my mind that counterpoint is counterpoint, when it corresponds with the general exposition of it which I have advanced, whatever the range, narrow or wide, of the harmonic basis upon which it is built; and I have sought to lead you up to the same point. My title says nothing about the rules of counterpoint, the teaching of counterpoint, the learning of counterpoint; contrapuntal training, or working, or exercises; but counterpoint itself, in modern music, free music. Those matters which I have just spoken of, but which are not included in my title, have to do with training, and are pedagogic; not a term of reproach, be it remembered. But having said thus much, it seems now the time for me to avow, without any hesitation or qualification, that it is my strong opinion, after passing as a student through the *curriculum* usual in those days, that of strict counterpoint; and, during some forty-seven years through the experience of a teacher, a trainer of students, with little deviation from the same method, though with enlarged apprehension of the purport and bearing of it all on music and musical composition as it now prevails among us; it is still, I say, my persuasion that the healthy solid course to be pursued, to form strong, clear musicianship, is that *curriculum* of strict counterpoint; with, however, the understanding that it is preparatory, disciplinary, and in view of the enlargement warranted, and inevitably to be attained, with our modern harmony systems. In short, it amounts pretty much to that distinction which my clear-headed, orthodox, but not narrow-minded friend, Dr. Pearce, has expressed between "student's counterpoint," and "composer's counterpoint." I must not now pursue this part of my discussion further; but have felt it incumbent on me, in justice to myself, and that you may understand my standpoint, to say thus much on this vexed and vexing question; which has been discussed recently so much, and sometimes with an acerbity which has seemed almost worthy of the old condemnatory denunciation of "*Mi* contra *Fa.*"

To proceed, then, on the understanding that

" Counterpoint " is to be interpreted as quite a different thing from a course of contrapuntal study and training; that counterpoint, in this sense, and as applied to " Modern, Free Composition," means much the same as that which is now so often spoken of as *polyphonic* writing ; I should say, in brief, that we mean, by " Contrapuntal writing,"—as distinguished from harmonizing—*independent part-writing*, upon whatever harmonic basis; by independent part-writing being meant, however, strong individuality, but still interdependence and co-operation for one common purpose, the production of a harmonious whole ; to use, with all reverence, a Scriptural illustration, " compact together by that which every joint supplieth ; " the idea of subordination being only so far included as in ordinary life, in conjunction with social courtesy : the independence of each being such as shall be subordinate to the well-being of all. Or again, that all shall be subordinate to the honouring of one ; that honouring of one being most signal when each and all recite his praises, deriving suggestions from his virtues. In taking a subject, which in counterpoint exercises is called a *Canto Fermo*, the counterpoint is avowedly suggested by whatever is in that subject, and so far, must be subordinate. The axiom has been enunciated: "no one ever said nothing well." And sometimes a subject is so barren of suggestiveness, or so awkward in the harmonic progressions which it is alone capable of that, after trying to "counterpoint it"—for we have got into the way of making a verb of the term, and of so describing the process—one has reluctantly to confess, " I can make nothing of it :" and so to illustrate the truth of the axiom. But it must be owned that the emphasis of that half-petulant confession should perhaps come on " I," rather than on " it," or on " nothing." Some are more susceptible of suggestion than others; just as the poet's eye, the artist's eye, perceive so much more in the objects of nature than others ; there are those to whom the primrose is, truly, " a yellow primrose," and exceedingly pretty as such ; but a great deal more.

And as, when all of a company are joining, and vieing with one another in the praises of any object of admiration, one utters a happy phrase which, striking on another's ears, is taken up and reiterated, with possibly some happy addition or embellishment, and again passed on imitatively,—so, in music ; that device of interest which we term imitation is an outcome of counterpoint; in its crude, rigid, form, as canon; in its most highly developed structural form, as fugue; in its applied use, as one among various methods of setting forth the resources of a theme, in the more or less partial or strict imitational devices that take their place in free composition. Now all this is " Composer's Counterpoint;" the composer's application of the principles—not subservience to the rules; use of the facility, putting forth of the strength, assertion of the freedom and mastery—acquired by the discipline of a patiently pursued course of contrapuntal study and exercise, within fetters, now exhibited in the enlarged domain of a wide tonal and harmonic system. Does anyone who understands and takes in the philosophy of counterpoint as I have stated it think of asking in the midst of it: "Is that allowed? is that according to rule?" The contrapuntally trained man, on emerging from his disciplinary course, is as a strong man rejoicing to run a race. The non-disciplined man is timid at every step, and is ever asking: " May I do this? will that be wrong?" He is not equipped as the other. He either stumbles, or else uses or mis-uses his so-called liberty, as a cloak of wayward license. When a student asks concerning his own work:

" May I do this ? Is that allowed?" he is taking the right position, as being "under tutors and governors." He is a learner; and if he says " Is this against the rule?" concerning such and such a matter, he of course must be assumed to refer to the rules given to him, as a learner, by his teacher. Now, of course, the rules about counterpoint, as about other things, were originally laid down, in the early days of the art, as a formulating of the opinion or judgment of an individual who gave special thought to the subject, or of the *consensus* of judgment of the best musicians of the period. And, therefore, they possessed just so much authority as might reasonably be assigned to mature and thoughtful judgment at the time, at the particular stage of advancement and culture then attained. But inasmuch as it was not as in a matter of research, and of fact, in which one who had given more thought to the subject had a right to speak authoritatively; but a matter largely of feeling; or in which one formulated a principle for other workers in one way, and another in another way, and in which some openness of view might well be permitted without any artistic excommunication; so, as the point of view shifted or varied somewhat, and the range of vision became gradually enlarged, *rules*, as expressions of judgment, individual or collective, would vary, would relax, and would less assume the attitude of authority.  So that when a student finds, in an acknowledged composer's work, an infringement of a rule that has been given to him to observe—though even in that, he may be mistaken as to the principle involved in the rule—and then asks : " Is that wrong ? " or " Is that allowed?" the first answer may well be,—"There exists no supreme authority with any sort of right to allow or disallow such a composer as the one whose work you have in hand ; such a one has earned and established his right to be a law unto himself.  It may not be allowed to you to do as he has done, because you have not proved or attained to the capacity which fulness of judgment alone can impart, to judge when that which to you is a rule may be departed from, perhaps without infringing the principle involved in that rule ; or, if not that, may be waived in favour of another principle, and for the securing of a higher end."  This statement of the case has, I am well aware, been animadverted on as tantamount to saying : " So and so is right for Mozart or for Bach, but wrong for you."  But the truer way of putting it would be : " Bach or

Mozart, in all probability, would not have done it, had it not been right and good, artistically, in the circumstances. In about equal probability—if you did it—you a student, it would be from mis-judgment, or from carelessness." At all events, do let us get rid of any talk as to whether that which Mozart, Bach, Beethoven, have written is *allowed:* whether in individual or collective opinion it be good or not. There is no court of appeal against their judgment. All this is said with full acknowledgment that even as " Homer may nod," so there may be found oversights, even in the otherwise perfect work of the great men of our art. It is not condoning of such lapses that is here contended for; only an understanding of how the question stands of authority and allowance; of Cherubini, Albrechtsberger and Co., against Mozart, Beethoven and Co.

At this point, however, you may with fair reason ask me what I mean by speaking of breaking a rule, and yet not infringing a principle; or, more useful still to consider, how far the principles of strict counterpoint may be said to be carried on into the wider domain of free writing as practised and understood among us nowadays. Because there is a great deal of loose, inexact talk, not only about counterpoint, but about other subjects of even more importance, in which such expressions as "the letter *versus* the spirit," or "the principle *versus* the rule," are used.   Now I venture to say that one strong characteristic of counterpoint is its antagonism to everything inexact, ill-defined, and, to use a colloquialism, "slip-shod."   In counterpoint there is, as expressed in the rules of strict counterpoint, a clear distinction, to be always indicated and acted on, between *essential* notes and *unessential* notes ; the distinction, in *strict* writing, being always associated with that between concords and discords ; obviously because the strict style recognizes no essential discords, no fundamental dissonances ; none but passing-notes, with slight modifications or varieties of these, as in the case of changing-notes and intermediate notes (this latter term being one for which, I believe, I am wholly responsible) and prepared discords in the form of suspensions.   Now this *principle*, with the definiteness as to harmony which it involves, may surely be carried out, though there may be all the additional resources at command which the evolution of modern harmony theories has opened up.   It means, in familiar language, no shuffling, no evasion, no equivocation as to what position, and power, and requirement attach to every note. And it means not merely that every note shall be explainable, but that it shall require no explanation, being self-explanatory in its mode of appearance, explanation often amounting to a process, not ingenuous, of explaining away the clear logical, or illogical meaning of the note. Surely you will not ask me to enlarge upon the way in which this principle may be carried out in free composition. No note must be inexplicable or unaccountable, but honestly assignable to a definite harmony; and it must never be, so to speak, lost sight of if it be of a nature which carries with it any responsibility. Counterpoint is the ally of clear, definite thinking, and unequivocal expression thereof. And it is strong, just in proportion as it not only can be assigned to definite harmony, but is expressive of that harmony, expository of it; somewhat after the manner, or according to the axiom of the robust writer of English who counselled that one should express oneself not only so that one can be understood, but so that one cannot be misunderstood. "Free counterpoint" does not mean "free-and-easy" writing, "anything you please," it means simply

enlarged scope, extended range, admittedly
fuller understanding of combinations and progressions not recognized by our older musicians.
But let not the crudity of antiquity be ex-
changed for the crudity of immaturity.   The
ancients, however limited or restricted we may
think their knowledge or understanding, at all
events *did* what they *knew*.   Can it be said that
the younger, modern musicians always know
what they do ?   Counterpoint of any kind should
expound, illustrate, and enhance the theme to
which it is added, showing how suggestive of
fine harmonies and progressions that theme is.
If the counterpoint itself needs expounding, it
has certainly missed its mark.

It has been inevitable, in what I have
advanced, that I have touched on the controversy which has been waging of late years
about strict *versus* free counterpoint ; but this
has been unwillingly, on my own part, not with
any intention to fan the flame, nor to act pre-
sumptuously as arbitrator or umpire between
the contending disputants, nor to issue a
*manifesto*, as though, forsooth, I had any right
to pose as authoritative.   I have rather had it
in my mind to show that the difference is one
about educational tactics, not about composition.

It is not a question of musical art in our present stage with regard to that art, but of training and study as to what course will best lead to the desired result. I have had in view not candidates at examinations, but aspirants after solidity and strength, combined with beauty, in musical composition. Therefore I have sought to recall the true nature of counterpoint, of what sort worthy the name; and the bearing of that, and, therefore, of contrapuntal training upon actual composition, as we now understand it, and, according to our ability, practise it. And I have spoken of the suggestiveness of contrapuntal study and writing as to the use to be made, the account to which may be turned such ideas as we may have; and how it will purify as well as solidify our writing. Even the lightest and slightest kinds of composition will be improved, not by the importation of contrapuntal passages which would be incongruously out of keeping with their style, but by the scrutinizing care about small details which becomes a habit of mind with those who undergo contrapuntal discipline, which scrutiny they will, almost unconsciously, exercise as they write. A trained grammarian need not, and should not, worry himself about grammatical rules as he talks,

M

however he may use them in the construction
of long or involved sentences in literary work.
As he speaks one should not have to say,
" How well he knows the rules," but " How
nicely he expresses himself." Contrapuntal
training should affect even the lightest, most
uncontrapuntal compositions ; imparting finish
and strength to them. Quite apart from any
question of harmonic basis in a waltz or similar
light piece, with merely supporting as distinguished from decorative or expository accompaniment, one shall see, or hear evidence of the
writer having hold of the principle brought out
in second and third species of not having consecutive perfect concords between successive
accents, or beginnings of bars, especially in
extreme parts, such as are so flagrantly irritating
not only in " barrel-organ " and " German band "
accompaniments, but in many printed compositions—if they may be so termed—of that
class. And, similarly, in *arpeggio* accompaniments to songs and the like, though *arpeggios*
are essentially uncontrapuntal—mind, I say not
unmusicianly—one shall see that those two
species, which have, of course, occasional
*arpeggio* bars intermixed with the passing-note
bars which constitute their distinguishing feature

and power, have permeated that form of writing.

I have used the terms "modern" and "free" composition in my title. The fashion, nowadays, is to characterize quite modern music as "romantic," and to contrast it with the "classical." But whether or not the romantic element is discernible in the classical and contrapuntal style, surely there is no reason why the most romantic writer should discard, instead of acquiring, the solidity, virility, stamina, finish, and law-abidingness which a thorough contrapuntal training is adapted to impart; or should disdain the suggestiveness as to the use to be made of subjects or themes by the varied modes of presentation which counterpoint work inculcates: inversion, as in double counterpoint; imitation, as in canon and fugue, and so on. These things need not hinder imagination; only guide and help it.

As to where strict writing may be said to have ceased, or merged into free — in other words, which is ancient music and which is modern—I will only here say that it is by no means a question of dates, periods, and sharp line of demarcation. It is customary to speak of Bach, and even of Haydn, as *Old* Masters;

but the harmonic system, whether or not formulated, yet certainly involved, implied, and illustrated, in Bach, is as modern, extensive, and free, as the most romantic could desire if he be willing to be orderly in conjunction with his romanticism.   All this might be illustrated at length, did time permit, and were means available.   I have, however, sought to set before you and to emphasize, the real philosophy of counterpoint, of any reasonable kind ; which is not a matter of strict or free, of rules or licences ; but holds good as the composer's *Thesaurus* of appliances.   The application and working out of that which I have advanced rests with yourselves.   I venture to hope that my treatment of a vexed question will prove suggestive and not vexatious.

—

# VII

# THE MUSIC OF THE VICTORIAN ERA [1]

" 'Tis sixty years since" that our gracious Queen—God bless her!—began to reign over us ; and we may truly say that she has " done that which is good," and that her character and example, her encouragements and her protests, her culture and her tastes, have been such as to stimulate and nurture the intellectual and moral, as well as the material and political well-being of the people—or, rather, the peoples—over whom her beneficent and constitutional sway has been extended. We look upon, and speak of, the whole period as less of a time of government and authority than of freedom and consequent development ; and we speak of it, therefore, less as a reign than as an *era*, THE VICTORIAN ERA, an era marked, undoubtedly, as all such lengthened periods must be, by undulations, not to say vicissitudes, but signally

[1] Delivered in the year 1897.

characterized by onwardness and upwardness in
the commonwealth.   For it has been a commonwealth under a mild but genuine sovereignty.
Just because of this, because the spirit of our
Queen has ever been one of consideration for
her people, reminding us of the shepherd-king
who spoke of the people as "these sheep,"[1] to
be tended, rather than ruled, the people do—
notwithstanding some churls and malcontents
—this year say and sing, "with heart and voice,
'God Save the Queen.'"   And we musicians,
what have we to say concerning this era, this
"golden age"?   What about our Art? has it
been stagnant, while all around has been living?
I trow not ; and am honoured by being asked to
review its progressive course during this happy
era.   "'Tis sixty years since."   Yes, but I have
not the pen of the author of "Waverley."
Could I wave the magic wand of that great
"Wizard of the North," I would enchain and
entrance you.   As it is, I have accepted the
task and pleasure with much diffidence,—that
of reviewing the progress of music in England
during these sixty years.   I may at least claim
one qualification, which should impart some
reality and life to my discourse, as it does

[1] 2 Sam. xxiv. 17 ; 1 Chron. xxi. 17.

impart interest to my own mind, namely, that a very considerable part of that which I have to relate or to discuss has come more or less under my own personal observation, has been within my own ken, and is treasured in my own memory. I remember Coronation Day in 1838; my father, violoncellist, was in the orchestra at Westminster Abbey on that day; the only day on which I ever saw him in a red coat and knee-breeches, details which greatly impressed me at the time.    And, since my whole life has been passed in a musical atmosphere, surrounded by musical people, and devoted to musical pursuits, the preparation of my address has not been a matter of "reading up" an unfamiliar subject, but of more or less exact verification of a host of memories, an arrangement of the gatherings of these many years, and the bringing to a focus the observations and reflections of a not very limited experience.    During the whole of that experience I have been watchfully and critically observant, and, I hope, accurate.    I have formed opinions of the tendencies of musical developments, the directions in which the art has moved; and, therefore, have not now, afresh, to formulate a philosophy of musical history.    Thus much with regard to my own fitness for the task that has been assigned to me ; any counterbalancing unfitness you will discover.

And now, with respect to the subject that is to engage our attention—music in England during the past sixty years, and, in connection therewith, certain idiomatic characteristics. To talk about the progress of English musical idioms during these sixty years would be narrowness and nonsense ; a history, were it true, of stunted growth, not of healthy life and enlargement. Music is cosmopolitan. Mankind were dispersed, and are much separated, by confusion and difference of tongues ; but music is one of the bonds of union, by reason of its universality, its oneness ; not a badge of national distinction, or separation, or independence ; and I am certainly not about to occupy your time and attention with any discussion of national peculiarities of musical dialect ; to engage in any profitless controversy as to whether we are or are not a musical nation, though a few facts bearing upon that question will come before us, nay, rather, the whole record bears upon it. My business is with the beautiful art of music, as it is felt and understood by cultured and susceptible minds of all climes : and, just now, among us, music as a part of our modern civilization. This

is as well to say, because, some years ago, a
writer on music—an Englishman, be it observed,
not a German—wrote to the effect that there is
no such entity now, if indeed there ever was,
as English music; that all the prominent young
composers in England are writing German music.
And, on the other hand, an American critic has
stated that, "to the older generation of English
musicians, music came to an end with Beethoven
and Mendelssohn;" and has expressed lack of
faith in the reality of that which he terms the
"boasted" musical progress of the English. How
do we stand now, in comparison with sixty years
since? And what have been the workings of
the musical community during that period? To
what extent, and in what ways, have we shared
in, kept pace with, the general current of musical
advancement? In replying to such inquiries, it
must be remembered that we cannot now plead
insularity; facilities of travel and communication
have broken down any barriers which might
seem to insulate if not to isolate us. And we
have neither wrought as an independent community, nor remained uninfluenced by the general
course of musical events.

Let us glance at the condition of musical
England, sixty years ago.

It would be interesting, did time permit, to trace the development of music in England from very early times, when it flourished amongst us, in the somewhat cruder forms of vocal part-music : the Madrigal School, the splendid array of church music by Orlando Gibbons, Henry Purcell, and many others ; to note the irresistibly overwhelming influence of the long residence among us of Handel, the almost paralyzing effect of his stupendous genius upon the pro-ductiveness of English musicians, though it must ever be an honour to us that the mighty master found our soil so congenial to the work-ings of his amazing productive powers. But, notwithstanding these glorious traditions, it cannot be denied that there had been decline. The madrigal had declined, and given place to a much inferior order of composition, the glee. Ecclesiastical music also declined, though congregational singing of a certain kind, not artistic, however fervent, became more general, especially in connection with the Evangelical revival brought about by the Wesleys and Whitefield. The decline, especially, perhaps, as regards vigorous productiveness, may be variously accounted for. It has been attributed to Puritan influence, also to that of the house of

Hanover, although we are now commemorating the excellent influence upon art and culture of the most worthy representative of that house. But if, with the increased facilities of travel, there had come about also a great increase of continental intercourse, and our insular self-containedness had been somewhat disturbed, and if, moreover, the commanding genius of Haydn, Mozart and Beethoven had somewhat overawed some of our own musicians, and arrested them in their own self-dependence, while showing the way to higher attainments, in new departments, so as to lull them into some temporary inactivity, there were not lacking signs of reviving life and aspiration.

The societies then existent among us were, first and foremost, the now time-honoured *Philharmonic Society*, then in its twenty-fourth year of noble enterprise ; several of its founders and original members being still living in the year 1837, the commencement of the era we are considering, notably J. B. Cramer, Henry R. Bishop (afterwards knighted by our Queen), Charles Neate, the friend of Beethoven, Sir George T. Smart, who, as a boy, had beaten the drums under Haydn's conductorship, François Cramer, Moralt, the viola player, who married Dussek's widow, Vincent Novello, William Horsley, G. E. Griffin, of "Bluebell" notoriety—all of whom I well remember—and Thomas Attwood, concerning whom it is here to be mentioned that, born in London in 1767, having sung as a boy in the Chapel Royal until his voice broke, travelled in Italy and Germany, studying under Mozart. In 1796 he became organist of St. Paul's Cathedral and composer to the Chapel Royal; subsequently, he received the additional appointments of organist to the Chapels Royal at Brighton and St. James's. He devoted himself to his duties with earnestness, and wrote a number of fine anthems, as well as other works. Two of these were anthems for the coronations of George IV. and William IV. respectively. He undertook a third such work for the coronation of our present most gracious Queen Victoria, but died, March, 1838, without completing it; although I read that the one composed for the coronation of George IV. was sung as the young Queen entered the abbey, entitled, "I was glad."

Another important institution at that time was that termed *The Concerts of Antient Music*, or *Ancient Concerts* as they were generally called, also the *King's Concerts*, established 1776;

one of the rules being that no music composed within the previous twenty years should be performed. At the commencement of the period that we are considering the conductor was Mr. William Knyvett, he having held that post since 1831. Subsequent conductors were Sir George Smart, Mr. (afterwards Sir Henry R.) Bishop, Mr. Lucas, the violoncellist and excellent musician, and Mr. Turle, it not being the custom then, as now in most societies of the kind, to have a permanent conductor for the season. Sir Henry Bishop was ultimately appointed conductor. The programmes were largely Handelian, varied, however, by excerpts from Bach, Purcell, Corelli, Gluck, Hasse, and others; subsequently Mozart's name was admitted, and Haydn's, and later on, even that of Beethoven. In 1847, at a concert under the direction of Prince Albert, the solo organist was Mendelssohn, who played Bach's fugue on his own name. In November of that same year, Mendelssohn died; I need not say, to the inexpressible grief of the whole musical world. Such concerts may have served a certain purpose of conservative protest against empirical radicalism, but could hardly survive the spirit of advancement then manifesting itself, and the concerts came to an end in 1848. Until 1841 the conductor presided at the organ; but, in that year, the two functions of conductor and organist were separated and Mr. Lucas was appointed organist.

Other societies in existence sixty years since were the *Choral Harmonists' Society*, an association of amateurs for the performance of choro-orchestral works, which gave concerts at the London Tavern, from 1833 to 1851, at not a few of which I was present, and in my boyhood sang songs at one of them. The conductors and the soloists were professional; the successive conductors were Vincent Novello, Charles Neate, Charles Lucas, and Henry Westrop. Another similar society was the *City of London Classical Harmonists*. There was also the *Societa Armonica*, founded ten years before the accession, which gave concerts of symphonies, overtures, etc., at the Crown and Anchor, Free-mason's Tavern, and Opera Concert Room. There was also the *Cæcilian Society*, established in 1785 for the performance of sacred music, and subsequently undertaking oratorio performances.

The concerts were held successively in Friday Street, at Plasterers' Hall, at Painters' Hall, Coachmen's Hall, Paul's Head, and finally in

Albion Hall, London Wall, as I remember them. The society was dissolved in 1861. With the exception of the Lenten performances at the Covent Garden and Drury Lane theatres, the only regular performances of the oratorios of Handel and Haydn were those of this society, unless, indeed, mention be made of the "Messiah," performed at the Foundling. Of similar origin was the *Sacred Harmonic Society*, established in 1832, in the vestry of Gate Street Chapel, Lincoln's Inn Fields; subsequently a most important society, its performances in Exeter Hall being, doubtless, remembered well by some of my hearers. Mendelssohn conducted his "Elijah" for the society—its first production in London—in 1847; Spohr, also, conducted his "Fall of Babylon," "Christian's Prayer," and "Last Judgment," and his 84th Psalm, the last written expressly for the society. There had also been founded, in 1834, the very useful *Society of British Musicians*, at which many works of the principal living English composers were introduced during its chequered career, which was terminated in 1865. It had a good library, commenced, I believe, at the suggestion of my father. I was a member from 1846 till its dissolution. Its place has since been occupied by the

*Musical Artists' Society*, of which I was one of the founders, in 1874; playing the very first piece at its first performance, my Fantasia dedicated to Sir G. A. Macfarren. It is still pursuing its course, endeavouring, notwithstanding much difficulty, to help rising artists to obtain a hearing.

Besides these societies for the performance of works of magnitude, there were also societies for the practice, in social fashion, of the vocal part-music for which the English have been so famous ;—the *Madrigal Society*, founded in 1741, and still existing ; the *Catch Club*, established in 1761, and still existing ; the *Concentores Sodales*, founded by Dr. Callcott in 1798, or, rather, the revival by William Horsley of a society founded by Dr. Callcott in 1790 ; every member of the *Concentores Sodales* who composed contributing a new canon on the day of his presidency : dissolved in 1812, but resuscitated in 1817, with Attwood, Horsley, Linley, Spofforth, Evans, W. Hawes, J. F. Walmisley, Smart, Goss, Bishop, J. W. Elliott, in company with whom I once attended one of the society's meetings : it was dissolved in 1847 ; the Glee Club, founded in 1783, for which was composed Webbe's glee, " Glorious

Apollo," and which was dissolved in 1857. At
the meetings of this club old Samuel Wesley
attended as visitor, and played Bach's fugues
upon the pianoforte, he having been mainly instrumental in introducing them into this country.
Moscheles, also, and Mendelssohn were among
its distinguished performing visitors. When
the dissolution of these societies is recorded, it
must be remembered that "the old order
changeth," other influences were at work, and
other developments of the art.

One of these was the cultivation of chamber
music for instruments. You will, of course,
bear in mind that there were no Monday
Popular Concerts in those days; in fact, little
in the way of popular performances of good
music of any sort, little that appealed to a large
public, at what are now known as popular
prices. The founder of quartet concerts has
only recently been taken from us (1894), all
honour to his memory, Joseph Haydon Bourne
Dando. He gave a concert in September, 1835,
entirely composed of such music, which, proving
successful, was followed by two more in the
October of the same year with increasing success. Mr. Dando, a *con amore* violinist of
excellent taste, then formed a quartet party

N

consisting, besides himself, of Henry Gamble
Blagrove, one of the most fascinating of English
violinists, who died in 1872; Henry Gattie,
another violinist of great excellence and intelligence, with regard both to music and other
matters, who, as a boy, supped with the author
of "Waverley," and was told stories by him,
thereby enabling him afterwards to discover
the authorship of the novels; and Charles
Lucas, the excellent violoncellist and all-round
musician, who died in 1869.   With them, to
the best of my recollection, was also associated
the excellent performer on the viola, Henry
Hill.   All of these, well known to myself personally, have now passed away.   The performances were commenced in 1836, and continued
annually at Hanover Square Rooms until 1842,
when Blagrove seceding from the enterprise,
Dando assumed the first violin, and the party
migrated to Crosby Hall, where the concerts
were continued in the Throne Room—in which
it was stated Sir Thomas More wrote his
"Utopia"—until 1853.   My father not unfre-
quently assisted as violoncellist; and, later on,
I myself as accompanist.   They were charming,
home-like concerts, being much in favour with
a *coterie* of City amateurs, who greatly relished

the quartets of Haydn, Mozart and Beethoven, who would hardly have sneered, as some modern City men, at the idea of rearing a generation of fiddlers.

As there were not concerts at popular prices in those days—the early years of the epoch which we are reviewing—so neither was printed music to be obtained without considerable outlay. A vocal score of an oratorio then cost at least a guinea, *folio* size, handy *octavo* editions not then being thought of, or, at least, *only* thought of. A single pianoforte sonata cost then as much as the complete set of Beethoven's thirty-two sonatas can now be obtained for. It is obvious that this was a formidable hindrance to the pursuits and progress of musical students who enjoy nowadays such unprecedented advantages in this and other respects.

There has been a large increase in the practice of *choral* singing, which, in the nature of the case, has been by bodies of amateurs. The impetus in this direction has been largely due to the establishment of singing-classes by Joseph Mainzer, who came to this country in 1839, and soon commenced the movement known as "singing for the million" (I remember being once present at one of his class-meetings); by

John Pyke Hullah, who commenced his classes on the adapted method of Wilhem at Exeter Hall in 1841 ; by Miss Sarah A. Glover, who first initiated the method known as the *Tonic Sol-fa*, her book on the subject having been published in 1845, and the system being afterwards adopted, with modifications, by the late Rev. John Curwen, Congregational minister, and further developed by his son, Mr. John Spencer Curwen, who has been fitted for that work by a professional training in the art of music. Into the much-vexed question of the merits of this system, as compared with that adopted in connection with the staff notation, I do not purpose entering. Suffice it to express satisfaction that, by any means, the love and practice of music among the people is extended. In connection with this widely-extended practice of choral singing, the number of compositions for that purpose has marvellously multiplied. Not only have a large number of cantatas and oratorios been produced, but likewise one form of composition for popular use may be said to have originated during this period, that, namely, termed the part-song. Not of so high a character structurally as the madrigal, and not requiring so high a training either for its per-

formance or for its comprehension or appreciation, the form has had a very wide popularity,
and has been produced in prodigious numbers
by a host of composers, good, bad, and in-
different, with amazingly fatal ease and rapidity.
The distinction between the part-song and its
much higher predecessor, the madrigal, now
well-nigh obsolete, is not difficult to describe.
Whereas a *madrigal* proper is essentially contrapuntal and imitational in structure and character, founded upon a few short phrases of
perhaps a very few notes each, responsively
treated between the parts, which move, not
simultaneously or consentaneously in notes of
about equal length, but with more or less of
intricacy and involvement, with little in the way
of rhythmical termination and division, few
closes, one part commencing as another finishes ;
a part-song, on the other hand, has few such
characteristics, the parts moving and finishing
together with simultaneous rhythm and phrasing, little " working," but largely consisting of
harmonized melody.    To write a good part-
song, a fair melodic capacity, original or otherwise, with tolerable knowledge of harmony, are
requisite ; but not much of power of continuity
or development, or that higher kind of part-

writing known as counterpoint.    These find
their scope in the madrigal, now not much
affected, any more than pure contrapuntal
writing of any kind.    A certain kind of prettiness and lusciousness in harmony is easier to
attain and to throw off; and, moreover, wins
instant acceptance.    Not so with the more solid,
serious manner of thinking, proceeding from,
and appealing to a higher mental condition.
Of course I am not in any way reflecting upon
the many beautiful part-songs which enrich our
anthology—in any such course I should re-
pudiate some of my own productions, having
written many part-songs—nor am I forgetting
the examples by German composers, Mendelssohn among the number, these having been by
some judged to result from an endeavour to
acclimatize our English glee, a very different
sort of composition, however.    But, returning
from our digression, I repeat that the *part-song*
is the product of our epoch.    With its rise not
only has the madrigal well-nigh disappeared—
this, indeed, it had done long previously—but
also its own immediate precursor, the glee, a
composition in at least two connected movements, to be sung not chorally, but by a single
voice to each part.

The various orchestral societies which I have mentioned appealed mainly to the few ; the prices of admission were, for the most part, prohibitive to the many.    But in 1838, the year of the coronation, an experiment was made of a more popularity-seeking kind, by a series of *Promenade Concerts*, given at the *English Opera House*, on the site of that now known as the *Lyceum Theatre*.    J. T. Willy was leader, and Negri, the singing-master, was conductor. These appealed to the public by the performance of light music ; the then public had not been educated into listening to high-class works.    In 1841, Jullien and Eliason commenced a similar enterprise.    Later on, Balfe, Mellon, and others have successively conducted such concerts ; but with the gradually extending transformation of character by the introduction of classical music, to the displacement of the dance-music element. To his honour be it recorded that Jullien, with all his charlatanry, did thus make an innovation so far as pecuniary prospects permitted, until, at the present time, a promenade concert could hardly be ventured upon without the classical element being included in the scheme ; and, moreover, a wholly classical concert of that kind is familiar enough among us : witness

recent enterprises at Queen's Hall and elsewhere.

Certain factors in the musical development of
our country during the period under consideration must be specially dealt with, and dwelt
upon; and one of the most important is the
influence of the visits of certain distinguished
foreign musicians. [This formed the subject of
one of Sir Sterndale Bennett's lectures while he
occupied the Chair of Music in the University
of Cambridge; though I am not sure whether
that particular lecture was not delivered at the
London Institution; perhaps only there. I did
not hear it, nor have I any knowledge of how
he treated the subject; so that the remarks I
make are quite independent.] It is impossible
to evade this consideration. We are tolerably
accustomed to the outcry against the undue influence of foreign encroachment, in music as in
other matters, and probably there has been, and
still is, more or less of justice in the complaint
of the preference shown to the foreigner above
the native. But even as our country is distinguished as the hospitable land of freedom, and
the refuge for all comers, so, with all our insularity, we have, I think it will not be denied,
always shown an eagerness to learn and profit

by whatever any visitors from foreign lands have been able to teach or bestow upon us. And I am not about to speak of the influence, beneficial or otherwise, of the horde of foreign teachers, competent or incompetent, who have taken up their residence among us, and vexed the indignant souls of natives who have felt aggrieved at being jostled and displaced by those whose superior claims to their own they have thought to have been too readily assumed. I have much higher ground than that to traverse. Even as it is our glory that, in the past century, our country was the adopted home of George Frederic Handel, and, by its demands and appreciation, gave that direction to his genius which resulted in the mighty series of works which have made his name such a household word among us ; so it is surely no confession of weakness, but our pride, that a marvellous, stimulating influence has been felt among us by the more or less frequent visits to our shores of such great artists as Spohr, Weber, Mendelssohn, and other composers of lesser, but still of no mean power, as well as by a host of distinguished performers, vocal and instrumental, some of whose names I shall have to specify.

It does not fall within my province to offer even the slightest sketch of the life and works of the first (chronologically) of the great artists I have mentioned, Louis Spohr, born at Brunswick in 1784, who did not, however, pay his first visit to this country until 1820. Although that year considerably precedes even the commencement of our epoch, yet as his visit was the first of a series, most interesting and influential, extending through a large portion of this epoch, up to the year 1853, I must thus begin at the beginning. "Dear old Spohr!" he has been called by more than one writer. At the first visit, in 1820, made at the invitation of our famous Philharmonic Society, he, one of the greatest of violinists, played on March 6th, his own concerto, "nello stilo drammatico," generally known as the Dramatic Concerto. Those who know it will not forget the long-sustained note with which the first solo commences. I have been told that the effect of that long-drawn-out note, with Spohr's fine tone, on its first performance was simply electrical upon the whole audience. This effect, moreover, would not be unaided by his striking personality, his stature being, I should think, several inches above six feet. I give simply my own rough estimate from tolerably vivid recollection, not of course of that occasion, but of subsequent visits. At the succeeding concert of the same season he played first violin in one of his own quartets, and at the third concert produced one of the finest of all his works, composed in London, his Symphony in D minor, a work which it is well-nigh impossible to hear without being stirred to enthusiasm. But, at that same concert, Spohr introduced something besides this splendid symphony ; he introduced or revived a custom which was then an innovation in this country, but since universally adopted. To those of my audience who years ago listened to orchestral and choral performances under what has seemed to them the almost magic wand of Costa, making the host of performers play as with the precision of one instrument, or, later, of the demonstrative Manns, of Richter, the self-possessed, and many others, it may seem almost incredible that such conductorship was not always the method of directing performances of that kind in this country. It was the fashion for the principal first violin player to *lead* the orchestra, while another musician sat at the pianoforte to *conduct*, by more or less continuous playing, alternating, I

suppose, with some beating and gesture with
the hand.   It need hardly be said that this
dual control, if control it might be called, did
not result in unity of performance or precision
of ensemble.   Spohr, on the occasion in question, notwithstanding some opposition, induced
the directors to allow him, instead of *leading*
the band with his violin, to *conduct* with the
*bâton*, and thus he introduced his beautiful
symphony simultaneously with his common-
sense method of controlling a body of performers, a prominent feature in this our epoch.
Spohr, however, was exceedingly pleased with
the Philharmonic orchestra, and said justly that
he gave the stringed instruments special work
in his symphony because of their special excellence.   I may be allowed to drop the hint that
in listening to large performances it is well to
remember that it is not the conductor who per-
forms the work but the players.   Recognition
of the importance of the functions of a conductor is one of the noticeable matters in connection with music or musical performance in
our epoch.   Costa was eminent for his general-
ship, his discipline of the forces under his
direction, not for the refinement of his musical
perception prompting his directions.   He dealt

in broad outlines, and what it is the fashion to call his *readings* were open to frequent challenge. Alfred Mellon, violinist and composer, was also . an excellent conductor; intelligent in intention, and efficient, though not demonstrative, in his method of expressing that intention. Sterndale Bennett, with the refinement of perception which always characterized him with regard to music that he loved, lacked command, daring, *verve*, just the qualities that distinguished Costa, who had none of the exquisite genius of Bennett. Besides Costa, who, though a Neapolitan, was resident among us, we have had foreign conductors on a visit to us, and conducting has been developing into a fine art during our era.

To return from this digression, Spohr's second visit to England was paid in 1839, within our epoch, to conduct his oratorio "Calvary" at the Norwich Festival, his popularity here having greatly increased, and the success of the oratorio was a genuine triumph. In 1842 another oratorio of his was produced at Norwich, "The Fall of Babylon," the *libretto* by Professor Edward Taylor, whom I remember, but Spohr was unable to be present at its production. Shortly afterwards, however, he for the third time visited us, and I then saw him conduct a performance of the " Fall of Babylon" in the Hanover Square Rooms, intended as a complimentary benefit to him, I believe, but certainly not succeeding in that intention, as the attendance was, from some cause, scanty, notwithstanding the high esteem in which he was held among us. The oratorio was repeated, on a large scale, by the Sacred Harmonic Society, at Exeter Hall; and the last concert of that season by the Philharmonic Society was largely devoted to his music and performance. Besides this, at the request of our Queen and Prince Albert, an extra concert, also devoted to him, was given that year on July 10th. In 1847 he visited London again, and at Exeter Hall " The Fall of Babylon," " The Last Judgment," " The Lord's Prayer," and Milton's 84th Psalm were produced. In 1852 he adapted his opera " Faust" to the Italian stage for performance at Covent Garden, where it was produced on July 15th, with small success however. His last visit to England was in 1853, in which year, at one of the Philharmonic Concerts, he was among the audience during the performance of, I think, his overture to " Jessonda," and I sat close to him. The whole room-full of listeners rose after the performance and turned towards the great man to render him obeisance. When, with some German phlegmatic reluctance, he rose to acknowledge their demonstrations of respect, his remarkable altitude was most noticeable; he was clearly seen by, though on the same standing ground as, the whole of the audience. I shall never forget the scene. The last time that I saw him was at a concert given by Molique, a violinist of the same school, when he was accompanied by Hesse, the well-known writer of organ music. I sat by them.

The influence of Spohr upon musical development at the early part of our epoch was very marked. He represented a splendid school of violin-playing ; and, by the charm of his writing for his own instrument, exercised a fascinating spell upon violinists. His concertos and quartets were great favourites with them. Moreover the mannerism of his compositions of all kinds, pretty generally acknowledged by all competent judges, a mannerism of harmonic progression and of modulating method which may be briefly characterized by the two words *chromatic* and *enharmonic*, was alluring, and not difficult to imitate ; and most of the then rising generation of composers came under the spell, caught

the trick, yielded to the most individualistic
influence of the time, and were very *Spohr-ish*
in their writing, until a yet more powerfully
seductive influence began to be felt.  But the
influence of Spohr, though it ceased to be direct,
was by no means unpermeating, and must be
reckoned with in any survey of the music of
the epoch.

The "yet more powerful" influence which
superseded that of Spohr was that of *Mendelssohn*.  That of Weber, indeed, had by no means
been slight, although he had been so little in this
country, in which however he died (in Great
Portland Street), in 1826, more than ten years
before the commencement of the epoch.  That
influence was strong upon operatic writing ; and
his *Invitation pour la Valse* may be said to
have originated the whole series of *Valses de
Salon*, whose name is legion.  Therefore his
influence cannot be left out of account in considering the music of the epoch ; it continues to
this day.  But that of Mendelssohn has been
much more universally felt among us, not only
from musical causes, but because of his frequent
visits to us, his engaging personality, and the
close intimacies he formed among us.

His first visit to London was in 1829, April

21st, when he was just turned twenty years of age ; and he lodged in Great Portland Street. He made his *début* before a London audience on the 25th of the following month, at a Philharmonic concert, when he conducted his Symphony in C minor, with a specially made new white *bâton*. The success was enormous; the slow movement receiving an encore which Mendelssohn declined ; the Scherzo, one that could not be resisted. A few days later he played at another concert ; and in June conducted his wonderful overture to "A Midsummer Night's Dream," for the first time in this country ; and, subsequently, played with Moscheles in his (Mendelssohn's) Double Concerto in E, for two pianofortes. His position amongst us was assured ; he was always a welcome guest. The nobility, diplomats, and society at large, at once honoured him. In that year he visited Scotland, where he planned the overture known as the "Hebrides," or "Isles of Fingal ;" and was first inspired for the "Scotch Symphony ;" also stayed in Wales, where he wrote three charming and well-known pianoforte pieces.

In April, 1832, he paid his second visit to England. During the season his "Hebrides" overture was performed, and he played his

o

G minor Concerto, both these at Philharmonic concerts. For a concert given by Mori, the violinist, he wrote and played his Capriccio in B minor for pianoforte and orchestra. He created quite a sensation, and, according to some, inaugurated a revolution in organ-playing by his performance on the instrument in St. Paul's Cathedral. And, in that same year, he here published, at Novello's in Dean Street, his first book of "Songs without Words." In the following year, 1833, he sent three works, according to commission, to our Philharmonic Society ; viz., the "Italian Symphony," the "Trumpet Overture," and "The Calm Sea and Prosperous Voyage" overture. He came to London to superintend the first performance of the symphony, which took place on May 13th. He subsequently paid a fourth visit to London, in company with his father, lodging all four times in Great Portland Street.

All this precedes our epoch, but is inevitably introduced. In 1837, however, when our epoch begins, Mendelssohn visited us for the fifth time, to conduct his new oratorio, "St. Paul," at the Birmingham Festival. The performance took place on September 28th, not the first production of the work in this country, but that at which it first definitely took hold of our people ; and no wonder that such a hold should then be taken, under the striking personal direction of the composer of the finest oratorio since Handel up to that time ; and some think it the finest, even now, placing it higher than " Elijah," which stupendous work was first talked over, and initiated and planned, here in London in that same year, in consultation at Hobart Place, Pimlico, with Mendelssohn's friend, Charles Klingemann.   At this same Birmingham Festival, 1837, Mendelssohn also played, for the first time, his second Pianoforte Concerto in D minor, and, on the organ, Bach's "St. Ann's Fugue." He also during that same visit to England played again at St. Paul's Cathedral, as also on the new organ then just erected by Messrs. Hill and Son in Christ Church, Newgate Street, under the direction of Dr. Gauntlett; thus adding his powerful influence to that of the Doctor in the direction of organ reform, especially in the matter of the C organ in the place of the G organ ; a technical distinction of great moment, well understood by organists, the prevalence now of the change being one of the important features in the musical development of our epoch.

The sixth visit of Mendelssohn to England was made in September, 1840, to conduct, at the Birmingham Festival, his recently-composed *Sinfonia-Cantante* (in other words, Choral Symphony), the "Lobgesang," or "Hymn of Praise," which had just been produced at Leipzig, and which has always been accepted as one of his greatest works. The success at Birmingham was enormous. At the same festival he played an organ fugue, and after the performance of the "Hymn of Praise," besides a private performance on the organ, he in the evening played his Pianoforte Concerto in G minor. At a subsequent concert of the Festival he extemporized on the organ, on themes from Handel's "Jephtha." Afterwards, in London, he played on Messrs. Hill and Son's new organ at St. Peter's, Cornhill, designed by Dr. Gauntlett, and then returned to Leipzig.

It is melancholy, in the midst of this record, to remember that all this constant production, work, and excitement were killing him!

In 1842 his seventh visit to England was made in company with his wife, to produce his long-in-hand "Scotch Symphony," which had been only recently brought out in Berlin, though, as I previously mentioned, inspired by his early visit to the Highlands. This was played for the first time in this country at the Philharmonic, on June 13th, I need hardly say, winning immediate acceptance. On the 27th of the same month, at another Philharmonic concert, he played his Concerto in D minor, now well known and liked by us, but which, Cipriani Potter told me—for I was not present—did not then make any great impression, possibly through Mendelssohn's fatigue after conducting, at the same concert, his " Isles of Fingal" overture. Subsequently, during the same season, he played on the organs at St. Peter's, Cornhill, and Christ Church, Newgate Street; and this was the year in which, by invitation, he paid two visits to our Queen and the Prince Consort, at Buckingham Palace, accompanying her Majesty in singing one of his sister, Fanny Hensel's, songs, published with his name, however; proffering the dedication to the Queen of the "Scotch Symphony," which was accepted, and so stands in the published copies, and received from her Majesty a beautiful ring, engraved " V. R. 1842." All this is charmingly described in one of his letters to his mother, together with his readily-accorded request to see the Royal children in their nursery.

The eighth visit which he paid to us was in 1844, when he accepted the invitation of our Philharmonic Society to conduct the last six concerts of the season. It was the same year which witnessed, moreover, the advent among us of Ernst, the violinist, Joachim, now so well-known and esteemed among us, then a lad of thirteen, and Piatti, now domiciled among us. I think it was in that year that Mendelssohn first produced among us the final version of his wonderful work, the "Walpurgisnacht;" though it must have been prior to that that a private performance of it took place, in which I, with my boy's voice, took part, the great composer himself accompanying us upon the pianoforte.

I think that it was in that year that, among the many concerts at which Mendelssohn appeared, was one by our own Sterndale Bennett, who was greatly esteemed by him, though not his pupil, as has been so mistakenly asserted; and at that concert he conducted his "Scotch Symphony," I sitting just by him, and he also playing, for the first time, with Bennett, his beautiful pianoforte duet, "Andante with Variations," in B flat, not published, however, till after his death, when two versions of it appeared

—one solo, the other duet, with some different matter peculiar to each form.

Moreover, in this year, 1844, took place one very notable appearance of Mendelssohn, that in which he, at one of Moscheles' concerts, played, with the concert-giver and Thalberg, Bach's Triple Concerto in D minor, for three pianofortes, on which occasion he made an extraordinary sensation by an *extempore cadenza*, introducing a wonderful octave passage, and creating a scene never to be forgotten. I was sitting behind him as he played, and narrowly escaped having to turn over for him, as he came near to where I was and said, " Who will turn for me ? " While I hesitated some one else volunteered to do it.

He visited us for the ninth time in 1846, to superintend the production of " Elijah " at the Birmingham Festival. Though I was not present at that first performance, I well remember the stir of enthusiasm which was aroused by that most popular of oratorios next to the " Messiah " and perhaps the " Creation."

Before his tenth visit—and, alas ! the last— he revised and re-wrote much of " Elijah," for he was very self-critical. In April, 1847, he came over, in company with Joachim ; and on the

16th, 23rd, 28th, and 30th of April, he conducted performances of it at Exeter Hall, the Queen and Prince Consort being present on the 23rd. He subsequently conducted it again at Manchester and Birmingham; conducted the "Scotch Symphony" and "Midsummer Night's Dream" overture at the Philharmonic, besides playing Beethoven's Concerto in G major, a performance which I had the felicity of hearing. He also played his C minor Trio, and some of his "Songs without Words," on May 4th at the Beethoven Quartet Society; on the next day, an organ fugue at the Antient Concert; on the 6th at the Prussian Embassy, and, after bidding farewell to the Queen and Prince Consort, left our shores on the 8th to go home, worn out, and die in the following November.

If it has seemed to you that I have taken a somewhat disproportionate time in speaking of Mendelssohn, considering that he was not an Englishman, and that I have had as my task, not to sketch Mendelssohn's life, but music among us during the epoch, I must remind you that I have *only* dealt, and that most inadequately, with his visits and appearances among us, his work among us as composer, pianist, organist, and conductor; and that it is

well-nigh impossible to exaggerate the potency
of the spell which he exercised over the musical
world here, and over musical students of that
time, who are the musical professors, and even
veterans, now. Other influences, again, have
arisen, and have more or less swayed the course
of thought and feeling, so that there is less of
the Mendelssohn vein, by a great deal, now,
than when his charming and irresistible personality were so magically felt among us ; and
even his " Songs without Words " are less played
than at one time. There will be reactions and
tides of influence in matters such as this. But
my brief glance at just what Mendelssohn did
among us—only that—could not be omitted, or
very well curtailed, consistently with any adequate
estimate of the music of the epoch. Briefly to
state these bare facts, that, at the commencement of our epoch, only one book of the " Songs
without Words " existed, just published, the rest
*were not;* now we have *eight sets :* the " Spinning
Song," or " Bees' Wedding," as it is called,
and the " Spring Song," as it is regarded,
did not exist; nor the "Scotch Symphony,"
nor " Elijah," nor the " Hymn of Praise," nor
" Lauda Sion," nor the "Walpurgisnacht," nor
some of the Psalms, nor the Organ Sonatas,

nor many other of the vocal and instrumental works so familiar to us; and it seems to us almost wonderful to think how people got on without them. And then think how rich our possessions now are in these works, and that so many have first of all originated or made their home among us, and of what he did for the organ and organ music, and of his marvellously beautiful pianoforte playing, which was such a delight and model to that generation, as I so well remember, though the healthy tradition of it has well-nigh died out. I repeat that it is impossible to over-estimate the Mendelssohn cult, as it may be called, as a factor in the music of our epoch, any more than to exaggerate the influence of Handel among us in the last century.

I will here mention two curious facts: one being that his first book of " Songs without Words," termed simply " Original Melodies," was published by Novello, in this country, at the composer's own expense; the other, that years afterwards, his now well-known Organ Sonatas were published by subscription, to insure the publisher against loss; and that one of the most eminent organists of the time not only declined to subscribe, but wrote an abusive letter

to the effect that there were many composers
equal to Mendelssohn, and so on, and so on.

I must now turn from these powerful influences from abroad, which, by their strong
individuality and by our own assimilative and
appreciative susceptibility, so greatly tended to
the maintenance and elevation of our musical
culture in the direction of all that is pure and
noble in art ; and consider what may be termed
a domestic influence, of wide-reaching character
which had sprung up among us, fifteen years
before the commencement of our epoch, and
was already beginning to bear fruit.   This was
the *Royal Academy of Music*, founded in 1822
by Lord Burghersh (afterwards Earl of West-
moreland), made at once the object of most
virulent attacks by the professors who were
not engaged in it, as designed, or at all events
likely to ruin the profession ; although its main
object was to train musical students of talent to
become competent professors, and as though
the ultimate advancement of the Divine Art
had not a prior claim to consideration to the
immediate personal interests of some of those,
perhaps not the best qualified, who were then
engaged in teaching.   Perhaps at that time the
Academy could hardly have been established

without some adventitious and aristocratic influence. But the aristocratic and autocratic amateur government under which it was placed was a constant disadvantage, though possibly of some advantage, to its welfare and success. Under the successive principalships of Dr. Crotch and Cipriani Potter it did excellent work in training and sending out through the country professors who had received something like a broad, general musical education, according to the then understood extent and nature of such a training. And such musicians were educated within its walls as these, who held honourable position for years in the profession, viz., Charles Lucas, Henry Blagrove (who afterwards also studied under Spohr, to extend and develop his style and attainments, and with excellent results), Charlotte Ann Birch, Charlotte Helen Dolby, Henry Brinley Richards, William Henry Holmes, James Howell, Kate Loder (now Lady Thompson), Agnes Zimmermann, William George Cusins, George Alexander Macfarren, Walter Macfarren, Charles and Thomas Harper, and a host of others. I myself was elected King's Scholar in 1846, and at the expiration of my scholarship in 1848 received the signal honour of a re-election to that distinction and privilege. On the expiration of the second period I was appointed Assistant-Professor, and shortly afterwards Professor, in the institution which I was proud to recognize as my *alma mater*, and have continued teaching therein ever since, a period of upwards of forty-six years. At the retirement of Cipriani Potter in 1859, Charles Lucas was appointed Principal; at his retirement in 1866, Sterndale Bennett was appointed his successor, with Otto Goldschmidt as Assistant-Principal; and on Bennett's death, in 1875, George Alexander Macfarren succeeded him, and worked with indefatigable vigour for the institution until his death in October, 1887, literally so, for, only an hour and a half before his death, he, blind and weak, dictated a complicated letter concerning its affairs.[1] The Royal Academy, notwithstanding that it has at various times been much handicapped, has struggled on to its present high position and prosperous condition, and has accomplished great things for music in this country. Much of the improvement in musical education is owing to its persistence in directing its labours to what is highest in the art.

[1] The present Principal, Sir Alexander C. Mackenzie, took office early in 1888.

The *Guildhall School of Music*, established under the auspices of the Corporation of London seventeen years ago, is now the largest musical school in the world. Its purpose, however, has been less to train artists and professors than to elevate the notions of music and musical education of those among whom such artists work, and to be the centre of sound instruction for the people generally. It may accomplish enormous good in that direction, especially now that it has as its principal a musician and a man of business.

*Trinity College, London*, is also working in the cause; and the more recently instituted *Royal College of Music*, succeeding the *National Training School*, is justifying itself in claiming public respect. Amongst them all, musical education ought not to be, and is not, at a standstill. All along the line, however, during our epoch, the veteran institution, the Royal Academy of Music, has been pursuing its way, with varying fortunes, from circumstances which cannot now be dealt with, but with unvaryingly healthy influence.

The *Royal College of Organists*, moreover, though not a training institution, must on no account be overlooked; especially as, in addition to its examination work, it has recently entered upon operations of a more educational kind.

And I must by no means fail to mention, in connection with this enumeration of our educational institutions, one which has a benevolent as well as a musical claim on our regard, the *Royal Normal College and Academy of Music for the Blind*, at which the pupils receive first-rate general as well as musical education.

And the various competitive schemes, such as the brass band contests instituted, I believe, by Mr. Enderby Jackson ; and the stimulating work in the Stratford Musical Festival, instituted by Mr. Curwen, all have a quickening effect upon the circles to which they appeal, and are among the agencies at work for good.

Just prior to the commencement of our epoch, there had emerged from the Royal Academy one who had been studying there for ten years, and had achieved much distinction ; who was one day to be Principal of the institution which had trained him ; was to be one of the glories of English music, and whose career and influence were to form an important factor in the course of the art among us. This was *William Sterndale Bennett*, son of a Sheffield professor, chorister of King's College Chapel, Cambridge, and afterwards so distinguished as a professor, pianist, composer. While yet a student at the Royal Academy he was specially noticed by Mendelssohn—a few years his senior—on the occasion of a visit that he paid to the institution; and his prophecy that he would make his mark was abundantly verified. The two geniuses became afterwards great friends, especially when Bennett visited Germany, where his beautiful pianoforte playing and his exquisite music were cordially received and appreciated. As I have previously remarked, Bennett was never Mendelssohn's pupil; and, still further, it is not wholly unnecessary to remark that the ignorant notion that Bennett was an imitator of Mendelssohn, and founded his style of composition upon that of the great German, is not only a mistake from a critical point of view, but also may be proved to be, so to speak, an anachronism, inasmuch as some of Bennett's most individual and characteristic works were produced, not only prior to his visit to Germany, when he might be supposed to be influenced by the great artist; but at a time when he had not had the opportunity of coming under any such spell, as over here the Mendelssohn mania, if I may call it so, had by no means set in at the time

when Bennett was studying, and developing his
own style, individuality, and genius. With
Schumann also Bennett was very intimate during
his stay in Germany, and dedicated to him his
Pianoforte Fantasia in A major; but he by no
means reciprocated the high estimate which
Schumann formed and generously expressed
concerning him ; " raved about him," is, I think,
the expression that Hans von Bülow uses.
Indeed, he depreciated Schumann as a composer ; he has done so in conversation with
myself.

To our *répertoire* of music for his own instrument Bennett added largely ; and, by his compositions of this class, has illustrated, as no one
else has, certain capacities of the pianoforte.
But then those who merely look at them in
print, without having heard him play them, can
form but little idea of the exquisite charm of the
two combined. I count it among my greatest,
happiest privileges as a musician, that I enjoyed
such frequent opportunities from my earliest
days of hearing his playing, as well as that of
Mendelssohn, which I expect never to hear
equalled. The style of pianoforte playing, even
in mechanical matters, has undergone no small
change since those days ; not, as those of us who

P

remember them think, in all respects a change
of real improvement.    There is now less of
charm, more of what is designated *technique*.
But I must not digress.

Bennett's other works consist of several
beautiful overtures,  " The  Naiads,"  " The
Wood Nymphs," " Parisina," " Paradise and the
Peri," etc., a symphony in G minor, his concertos for pianoforte and orchestra, as well as a
sestet for pianoforte and stringed and wind instruments ; a trio for pianoforte and strings, a
sonata for pianoforte and violonçello, composed
for Piatti ; the cantata, " The May Queen," the
short oratorio, " The Woman of Samaria," full
of beauties, and other works.

I think, perhaps, the "Woman of Samaria"
has failed to win the estimation to which its
beauties entitle it, partly from a lack of dramatic
interest, and this partly accounting for a similar
lack in the musical structure ; though it must, I
think, be admitted that this was a defect in
Bennett's own organization.

As Principal of the Royal Academy of Music,
he wrought excellent work, making much-needed
reforms, and rousing much sympathetic musical
interest in pupils and professors alike.

As professor in the University of Cambridge,

I am not aware that he effected much, though during his holding of that chair he wrote his Installation Ode, and a fine anthem for St. John's College Chapel.

Contemporary with Bennett, as student and professor, was another musician who has been a notable figure with great influence for all these years, George Alexander Macfarren, previously mentioned. This truly remarkable man, who by his theoretical teachings has largely directed the musical thought of students for so long, was born in 1813, three years earlier than Bennett, and survived him twelve years. I need not now detain you by a lengthened record of his services to music. But these two men have, among our own musicians, been the most prominent in the conservation and advancement of the art among us.

I can hardly pass from this brief reference to Macfarren without adverting to a feature in the course of our art during these years, one suggested by his career. Were I addressing a general audience I should hardly think it expedient to touch upon any technical point; but addressing the members of so distinguished a society of musicians, I have neither right nor occasion to evade even an esoteric matter. We

all know how involved Macfarren became in
controversy through his strenuous advocacy of
a certain theory of harmony ; and it has been a
characteristic of our era to engage in discussion
about various questions connected with our art,
theoretical, practical, acoustical, æsthetical, with
a view, apparently, to some finality of settle-
ment ; but I need hardly say, without arriving at
that result : *desirable* result, shall I say ? hardly,
perhaps ; unless, indeed, we are disposed to
ask, with Mendelssohn : " Why do people talk
so much about music ? why do they not, instead, write good music ? " The latter half of
the inquiry is not difficult to answer ; and perhaps that answer may suggest some reply to
the former half.   But we have had not merely
abundance of books for the use of students, but
abundance of more or less polemical treatises,
lectures, meetings, discussions about systems of
harmony, with or without acoustics ; methods of
teaching counterpoint ; bad ways of teaching
harmony ; pitch ; temperament ; absolute music
*versus* music-drama ; romantic *versus* classical ;
Tonic sol-fa ; movable Do ; Staff notation ;
above all, singing, and voice production ; in
connection with which I might give a list of
names such as Parkinson, Hewitt, Pole, Ellis,

Hiles, Day, with Macfarren, Stainer, Lunn, and a host of others, all anxious to contribute their *quota*, in most cases thinking that theirs would be the final touch settling the point once for all. When I once spoke of a particular theory of harmony as being still *sub judice*, a musician whose memory we many of us cherish very pleasantly, said to me : " Oh dear, no ! not *sub judice;* you cannot say that after the articles that I wrote in such a paper." Well, well ! I suppose it is all a sign of life, so long as we can carry on our discussions without asperity, or implication of incompetence on the part of those who differ from us. We aim at truth.

But, in addition to all this, there has been a vast contribution and addition to our musical literature, apart from controversy; valuable works, theoretical, philosophical, historical, biographical, æsthetic; in the truest sense, educational ; in fact, as I have termed it, *literature* in connection with our art. It is a false use, an unfortunate mis-appropriation of a term, to call music written for the pianoforte, for instance, the "literature " of the instrument. Literature has to do with books, though there are many books which do not come under the denomination. But I allude to such books as Parry's

"Art of Music"; his "Studies of the Great
Composers"; Macfarren's "History of Music
critically discussed"; Morton Latham's "Ren-
naissance of Music"; the many biographies of
musicians, etc. And it is a testimony to the
advance of interest in the subject that it should
have been deemed hopefully practicable to prepare and issue so ample, though still far from
complete a work as Grove's Dictionary.

And, in close connection with the discussion
characteristic of our time, the establishment and
continued vigour of the *Musical Association*
must also be recorded with gratulation. All
these things are indicative of the growing general
culture of musical men, without which, indeed,
all talk about the refining and elevating influence of the art itself is vain. Some recognition
of the fact of this elevation is evinced by the
larger number of our fraternity who have been
the recipients of knightly honours at the hands
of our gracious sovereign.

And of specially educational works it would
not be difficult to make a tolerably long list,
even of such as have been issued within a
comparatively short period; such as those of
Macfarren, of the late Rev. Sir Frederick Gore
Ouseley, of our own honoured member, Pro-

fessor Prout, and many others. On special subjects again, there are those on the Organ and on
the Pianoforte, by, respectively, Dr. Hopkins
and Mr. Hipkins. Truly it has not been an
unfruitful era in diligent research and literary
activity.

I must not omit, however, a further tribute of
respect to one to whom both Bennett and Macfarren, myself, and so many more of us musicians
owed so much for sound instruction, wise counsel,
high stimulus, generous friendship ; the father of
us all, Cipriani Potter ; the pupil of Attwood, of
Crotch, of Woelfl, and others ; in addition to all,
informally, of Beethoven. By his admirable
teaching both of the Pianoforte and of Composition, he formed the style of many a young artist ;
always inculcating excellent methods of touch,
opposed to all mere mechanical show and charlatanry ; always expounding the true principles of
structure and design in musical writing. He introduced several of Beethoven's works in this
country, and was always their advocate in the
days when some of the old-fashioned musicians
did not so unequivocally welcome them. Beethoven himself said of him, in one of his letters,
March 18th, 1818 : " Potter has visited me
several times ; he seems to be a good man,

and has talent for composition." His position as Principal of the Royal Academy of Music for so many years, enabled him to exercise a salutary, elevating influence, both on musical training generally, and on a large number of students individually; all yielding, willingly and irresistibly, to an influence that was as genial as it was classical, pure, and wide. His own music has fallen into undeserved neglect, except his excellent Pianoforte Studies, which are still justly valued. I need hardly say with what pride and pleasure I look back upon my intimate relations with a man so distinguished, personally and relatively.

There is one cult, or revival, of a noteworthy kind, which has characterized the last thirty-five or forty years, namely, the attention given in this country to the music of the great Leipsic cantor, Johann Sebastian Bach. Up to about forty-five or fifty years ago, even musicians were very little acquainted with any of his marvellous works except the forty-eight preludes and fugues for the pianoforte, and a few of the organ fugues; and even musicians, to a considerable extent (perhaps from their having, after all, only a slight acquaintance even with these) largely considered them rather as unmelodious, structural curiosities, than as real musical inspirations. In Germany, however, through the zeal of Mendelssohn, and in England through that of Sterndale Bennett, interest was awakened not only in some other printed works by the matchless master, but in many lying in manuscript in Germany, and there brought to light. In Germany a scheme for the publication of these unknown treasures has been actively carried on for a number of years, and in England, about forty-seven years ago, Sterndale Bennett was instrumental in establishing in London a Bach society, of which I was one of the earliest members; not for the publication so much as for the performance of, and for stimulating interest in, the wonderful music which had been so long neglected or mis-judged. In connection with this society, some of Bach's Motets and the St. Matthew's Passion-Music were published, and performances, under Bennett's direction, also took place. The society, after some years, was dissolved, but not without having done much of what it purposed doing. This is evidenced by such facts as that whereas, forty years ago, it was a rare thing indeed to see Bach's name in a programme except, indeed, at the Antient Concerts, or at Moscheles' historical performances on the piano-

forte and its precursors, and *never*, one may
say, was any work of his to be seen on an un-
professional person's desk.   Now it is the rule
rather than the exception, to have some Bach
music included in any season's list of musical
societies, and in almost all popular collections
of even teaching music, some of his pianoforte
pieces are included.   Moreover, since the dissolution of that society, another society has
arisen, the *Bach Choir*, who have given some
excellent performances of the Grand Mass in
B minor, and other works of Bach, though,
latterly, they have departed considerably from
their original policy and practice, and have performed a number of more or less unfamiliar
works, new and old.   The germ of all this real
or professed interest in such stupendous works
as these of Bach was the original *Bach Society*,
and although, like a number of things in modern
so-called culture—the æsthetic craze and so
forth—there is much affectation, and fashion,
and dilettantism about it, the influence is so
thoroughly good, without alloy, of the increased acquaintance with such classics, that
albeit it grows up side by side with so much
that is extravagant and sensational, one cannot but rejoice, feeling that things can hardly

go very far wrong while Bach is known and honoured.

One curious effect of the acquaintance with some of the lighter works of the grand old master has been that whereas, according to the custom of his time, his *suites* consisted mainly of the then prevalent dance measures, modern composers have begun to write in those measures—gavottes, bourrées, and the like—although the dances are obsolete, and there is no appropriateness or inspiring motive in the perpetuation.

I think I have placed before you some of the leading influences upon musical art among us that have given it much of its direction and character during the past sixty years. There has been our readiness to welcome, and to adopt, any good thing, from whatever source, responded to by the visits and work among us of Spohr, Mendelssohn, and, in a smaller way, Weber. And there has been the establishment of a Royal and National Academy of Music, with such excellent direction as that of Cipriani Potter, nurturing among us men like George Alexander Macfarren and Sterndale Bennett, upholding, perpetuating, and advancing the true and the pure.

But there have been subordinate influences at work. A host of lesser, though unquestionably eminent, musicians, have more or less frequently visited us, and exhibited some speciality of executive skill, or some idiosyncrasy or eccentricity, or really solid qualities, in performance or in composition, which have, for good or for evil, made their mark, and in some instances left that mark upon our style of performance, or our tastes in musical composition. And some of these have taken up their residence among us for a more or less lengthened period, and have exerted, so to speak, a leavening influence. Such a one, notably, was Ignace Moscheles, who resided in London from 1826 till 1846, and by his fine pianoforte playing, his conducting at the Philharmonic, his excellent teaching, his concertos, his admirable studies for the pianoforte, and his constant upholding of the highest in the art, won universal respect and was a power for good among us. I remember him well; and how, after years of absence, in 1861, he re-visited us in his old age, and though very nervous, as he, or his wife rather, details in his biography, re-appeared at a Philharmonic concert, in Hanover Square rooms, the scene of his early triumphs, and, amid indescribable enthusiasm, played, even then with marvellous fluency and power, his concerto in G minor.

Less healthy, but still, upon the whole, perhaps, of some influence for good, were the frequent visits of Sigismund Thalberg, a marvellous pianist, who, so to speak, founded a school of pianoforte playing and writing, exhibiting some resources of the instrument, and methods of performance, tending to develop those branches of the art, but needing care lest the fictitious element should degenerate into charlatanry.  But not to have heard Thalberg would have been a great loss.  He had an exceptional hand and altogether exceptional powers, but shone not in the intellectual qualities that are requisite in a musician.

His contemporary, Liszt, also a marvellous player, wrought, by his extraordinary powers, such havoc among all the good, classical traditions of pianoforte playing and pure music, although he began as a classical pianist, when a boy, that, undeceived by the glamour that has seemed to surround his remarkable personality, one who loves the true, and the good, and the beautiful, can only deplore a career which has corrupted the taste of so many young artists.  His influence seems to have been wholly pernicious.

Many players of what has been termed the "fire-eating" or "fireworks" school have appeared during the last fifty years, exciting some wonderment, which those who felt it mistook for musical appreciation, even as they mistook the performers for musicians, and the pieces for their display for music.  A more healthy tone prevails nowadays: although there will always, in every department, be those who aim at, and those who are caught by, sensationalism.  And, moreover, under the head of "higher development of pianoforte playing," there has, as I have hinted, been an amount of attention bestowed upon what is termed "technique," of late years, —I will not say excessive, but which has somewhat tended to render the fingers automatic, to the forgetfulness of that exquisite sensitiveness to the promptings of an informed mind, and a refined perception, which is one of the charms of true musical performance of all kinds.  But we must all acknowledge the debt that we owe to players like Madame Schumann, Rubinstein at his best—for sometimes he was at his worst —and some others for the almost revelations of certain works which they have signalized, so to speak, by their playing. And while we have among us so intelligent and true a pianist as our own fair young countrywoman, Miss Fanny Davies, we may wellnigh dismiss from our minds the apprehensions which might arise as to the effacement of what we have been accustomed to admire as genuine playing.

During these sixty years, moreover, many English composers have lived and produced: *John Barnett*, whose opera, " The Mountain Sylph," libretto by Thackeray, was successful, in 1834, the trio, " The Magic-Wove Scarf," being still included in concert programmes; *W. M. Rooke*, who wrote the opera " Amalie," 1837; more eminent still, *Michael William Balfe*, composer of " The Siege of Rochelle," " The Bohemian Girl," " Satanella," and many others. *Vincent Wallace*, composer of " Maritana," " Lurline," and other works; *Henry Smart*, nephew of Sir George Smart, who, besides an opera, " The Gnome of Hartzburg," a cantata, " The Bride of Dunkerron," and other cantatas, is as much esteemed for his excellent organ music as he was for his organ playing; *Edward James Loder*, composer of " The Night Dancers," " The Island of Calypso," and very many other works, among them being the well-known song, " The

Brave Old Oak"; *Charles Edward Horsley*, son of the glee-writer, and many other composers, now passed away, except, indeed, the veteran *John Barnett*, still residing at Cheltenham. And, in the department of organ music, organ playing and teaching, and church music, I must also mention a name which is here held in deserved honour, that of Dr. Edward J. Hopkins, organist of the Temple Church, still, happily, living and working among us.

But it must be owned that, with themselves, has to some considerable extent passed away the interest in their works. Why that which has once awakened interest should have ceased to do so, as though "a thing of beauty" were *not* "a joy for ever," is a question much too perplexing for me to enter into. Those who are disposed to pursue the subject will find it discussed with no little acumen in Browning's "Parleying" with Charles Avison. But there is no doubt of the fact that, except in the case of the very highest classics, there is such a decadence, and that "the old order changeth." We have now active among us a number of composers, young men, or at least not past middle life, who are producing works of quite a different kind, animated by quite a different spirit, untraditional, unconventional, aspiring, I must not say speculative or daring, but, at least to some extent, experimental ; informed less by the spirit of Mozart, or of Beethoven, or of Mendelssohn, than by that of Schumann, that of Chopin, that of Wagner, that of Brahms, in varying degrees. For these are the names to which the younger generation are turning. Thirty-five or forty years ago, little was known in this country of the works of Schumann, and that little was regarded with scant favour by the majority of staid, orthodox musicians. Now we gladly see his name in the season list of every series of concerts.

Another name has to be mentioned, of one whose acceptance has been slower, indeed, but very sure, because of the solidity, earnestness, profundity of his writings—the name which, during the preparation of this paper, represented a living composer, but now has to be uttered, not, indeed, with any of the tolerant reserve with which we sometimes speak of the dead, but with the hushed reverence due to one who indeed still speaks, and of whom, without any reserve, we may predict a growing appreciation, wherever single-mindedness, high think-

Q

ing, profoundness, solidity, earnestness, resolute disregard of all that approached the *ad captandum*, are reverenced. In grateful respect to him, for he has left us the " German Requiem," among many enduring works, let us name Johannes Brahms.

Of Wagner and the Wagner cult I am not desirous of speaking at any length, because the question is one not by any means wholly musical, but having to do with the alliance of music with other arts or accessories, so as to form one composite art; at least, this is how I understand the matter. Moreover, if the question is of the stupendous magnitude which Wagnerians contend, it cannot be dealt with adequately in a few crisp sentences. If it be not so, then it is hardly worth while to occupy time in discussing a delusion; and finally, since, avowedly, it has to do with the " music of the future," and my work to-night is with the past, or at most with the present, I am quite content to leave to the verdict of the future the validity of Wagnerian theories and claims, and can only hope that when, sixty years hence, the music of this epoch is reviewed, this question, if it then survive, will be dealt with with more ability and eloquence than I can now command. I will only say that there are two distinct issues : one being the question of music being able to stand alone, or whether she is, so to speak, used up, having said all that she can by herself and by existing methods ; the other question being the genius or otherwise of Wagner himself as a musician : I refer to him in no other aspect. But there is one effect which the rise and development of Wagner's dramatic or operatic theories have had which is not a matter of regret, viz., the calling attention to the vapidity of much of that which is known as Italian opera, as represented by Rossini—although his genius must be freely acknowledged—and his followers, Bellini, Donizetti, Verdi, and others. My time has not permitted me to enlarge upon the various phases of operatic music, which, moreover, are not a matter of music pure and simple, but involve considerations much too extensive for the present occasion.

Of one thing there is no question, that Wagner and his theories and manner have greatly affected or infected the younger race of musicians.

François Fréderic Chopin, Polish musician, composer and pianist, of unquestionable, though limited genius, although he visited this country, and in enfeebled health played at the Guildhall, at a concert for the benefit of Polish refugees shortly before his death in 1849, influenced young English musicians, not by his presence and performance, but by the individuality and charm of his music.   In developing power, the production of large works, all that goes to make up greatness, he was deficient; but he had a vein of thought, or sentiment rather, of his own, which appeals to certain susceptibilities; and, like everyone who has really something of his own originating to say, has secured his own niche among original composers, and his influence in imparting a certain colouring, or tone, or sentiment, to contemporary composition is undeniable.

Schumann, in like manner, though to some extent influenced by Beethoven and by Mendelssohn—who has *not* been since their time? —had also a phase of thought and feeling of his own; his composition was not reproduction: so that, notwithstanding defects upon which I cannot now enlarge, it has certain vitality.

And the English composers of this generation, no longer marked or fettered by the insularity and self-containedness of the time anterior to that which we have been considering, but keenly alive to all external influences, quick to assimilate, eclectically, whatever finds affinity in their own minds, but withal having English characteristics of their own, are writing —not, as was said by some critic a few years ago, German music, nay, nor English music, but *music*. They are expressing " the spirit of the age," very hard to define or characterize, in artistic matters. They are, somewhat defiantly, almost petulantly, throwing off what they esteem pedantic fetters, ridding themselves of what they think antiquated formularies or formalities, even forms, and are, so to speak, exploring, launching out, experimentalizing—shall I say annexing and colonizing ?—and thus exhibiting English characteristics. While we have among us writers with the enthusiasm and ability of Arthur Seymour Sullivan, Alexander Campbell Mackenzie, Frederic Hymen Cowen, Charles Villiers Stanford, Charles Hubert Hastings Parry, and others who show their English nationality, not by insular narrowness, but by their all-embracingness, we may well believe and hope that upon English music, as upon the British empire, the sun will never set, until the cataclysm occurs that shall bring the New Zealander to the ruins of London Bridge.